A Thug & His Queen

What Wouldn't You Do?

An Urban Hood Romance

Tamicka Higgins

© 2015

Disclaimer

This is a work of fiction. Names, places, characters and events are all fictitious for the reader's pleasure. Any similarities to real people, places, events, living or dead are all coincidental.

This book contains sexually explicit content that is intended for ADULTS ONLY (+18).

CHAPTER 1

Ronnisha was living what many in the hood would call the dream life. Having grown up like many urban, black children, she too had to make her way out of an unstable upbringing. She was raised by her aunt, but her father would pop up every so often and act as if he wanted to be a father. There would be other times where the man did little to nothing to hide the fact that Ronnisha was the child that he really didn't want – the child that Ronnisha's mother had tried to use to trap him back when they were just barely out of high school. Ronnisha always found some irony in that situation, especially when her mother was the one who ran off to be with another man while her father at least made sure a few things were taken care of.

As if her upbringing was not hard enough, Ronnisha also had to deal with the negative effects of what many would call a gift: her looks. To say the least, Ronnisha was beautiful. In elementary school, middle school, and high school, Ronnisha was always considered to be one of the baddest chicks in every school she attended. While many people would have let such compliments go to their head, in many ways Ronnisha could credit her upbringing as the reason she was so humble. At the same time, she never hid or downplayed her beauty. Even though there were times Ronnisha's looks would cause envy in other chicks, especially if those chicks' dudes were caught looking a little too hard in her direction, Ronnisha could handle herself quite well. In fact, growing up in one of Indianapolis' worst hoods, it wasn't uncommon for her Aunt Kim to come out onto the porch and look down the block to see Ronnisha wearing some girl out on the corner, sometimes as soon as they got off the bus, because she'd get a little too deep into her feelings.

As Ronnisha got older, and had become more committed to being that ride or die chick for her man Danez, she had cooled her temper somewhat. At 5'2" in height, Ronnisha had what her grandmother would call, before she passed away, perfect brown skin. Throughout her teenage years, she was lucky enough to be one of the few kids in high school who didn't have to worry about too many pimples popping up on her skin. And she was smart enough to read up early about the different lesser-known remedies she could use to keep the skin on her face from scarring up when she did get a pimple or a light scratch in a fight. Ronnisha also prided herself in being that one black chick in school that nobody ever saw wearing hair extensions of any kind. Her long black hair was thick and luscious and only complimented the fact that her brown skin was so smooth. Her lips were full and her eyelashes were the definition of feminine. Ronnisha's bright eyes were often the prize of her looks, at least in the face.

When it came to Ronnisha's body, she simply had it going on. Since turning sixteen years old, she had developed into a very well-shaped woman. In fact, she had a body that some women would pay for and stay in the gym more than church to keep up. While many of her friends and peers may have struggled to keep a boyfriend, Ronnisha had her pick of the crop. She could pick and choose, if she wanted to. Not to mention, they were drawn to her like a magnet, even when she'd be at a store on a Sunday morning and not dressed her best, dudes would still try to get at her. Her ass was big and round, but not silly looking. The 22-year old's waist was small and her double D chest was perky and full. And she only showed it off more by wearing shirts that were low cut.

Ronnisha passed a blunt to her girl, Tyne, as they sat in her and Danez' luxury apartment downtown. Even though Ronnisha had been living in the eight-floor apartment building with Danez for a little over a year, there were still times she struggled to believe that she lived in a place with a doorman – that she lived in a place with a view of the skyline and a balcony and stainless steel appliances. She loved being able to have her girl Tyne over, especially since the two of them had been the best of friends since they met in first period the first day of their freshmen year of high school. Tyne smiled as she grabbed the blunt, having arrived about an hour ago to just stop by and see her girl Ronnisha on her way home from work.

"Girl, so what you sayin'?" Tyne, who was tall and thin and very model-like, much like the singer Ciara, asked. "You sayin' that I need to have you approve him first?"

Ronnisha shook her head and smiled. "Naw, girl," she said, responding to Tyne's question about whether or not Tyne was dating the right guy right now. "You know me, girl. That is not what I'm saying at all. That ain't even something I would say. All I'm sayin' is that before you talk about moving in with this nigga, I think I should at least meet him and tell you what I think so you can know."

"Who you supposed to be now?" Tyne asked sarcastically. "Miss *I know how people should handle their relationships.*"

"Girl, please," Ronnisha said, leaning her head onto the back of the black leather couch where they sat. "Don't take this the wrong way, girl, but I know that you probably will, but I feel like I need to help you. I need to be your Red Cross for these niggas you be datin' and need to be saved from."

"My Red Cross?" Tyne asked, moving her neck to the side. "And what the fuck make you say that?"

Ronnisha looked dead at Tyne and said, "Girl, you know why. Think about it. At the rate you goin', I'mma have to start fillin' out nicknames for the niggas that you be seein' and stuff. By the time I learn one dude's name, next thing I know, he out the door and you talkin' about somebody else that you done met and how he might be the one and this and that and this and that. Girl, you lost and you know it."

"Ronnisha, girl, I am not lost," Tyne said, passing the blunt back to Ronnisha. "If anything, I'm the one that is found and your ass is lost. I don't stay with no nigga unless it's working out for me. If the shit ain't working out, then I gotta bounce and not waste my time."

"So," Ronnisha said, "about this new nigga. What's the deal? What prison you find him in?" She paused then added, sarcastically, "Let me get my notebook so I can take notes and stuff on this one. Girl, who am I kiddin'? I might as well go on and get some folders for you and one of them little short filing cabinets."

Tyne squinted at Ronnisha then cracked a smile. "Ha, ha," she said, flatly. "Girl, you really think you funny. Anyway," she purposely smacked her lips together loudly, "his name is Shannon and he from Detroit."

Ronnisha looked at Tyne with a serious face. "Detroit?" she asked. "Oh Lord. You done went and got you one of them savages."

Tyne burst into laughter and leaned over to slap Ronnisha's leg. "Girl, don't say that," she said. "You ain't even met him yet. For real, though. He is really nice and stuff, I swear."

Ronnisha looked at Tyne with skepticism. "Girl, I know I'm dating a hood nigga," she said then smiled. "But you like them niggas that you see on America's Most Wanted and stuff. I bet I can describe this new nigga you got."

"Go ahead," Tyne said in a daring way. "Go right ahead."

"Okay," Ronnisha said, touching her chin. "I know the nigga already got a baby."

"And so do yours," Tyne said.

"Okay, okay, girl," Ronnisha said. "Calm down. How many he got, though?"

Tyne looked away with a smirk on her face. Ronnisha pressured her by forcing herself to cough. "Okay, he got three," Tyne said. "But that don't make him a bad person. Yours got one. What's the difference?"

"How many baby mamas?" Ronnisha asked. "Tell me that."

Once again, Tyne hesitated before answering. "Okay, three," she said. "But he used to date them trap queen type of chicks. He done with all that. I mean, look who he datin' now."

"Hmm, hmm," Ronnisha said. "I already know he a dark skin nigga."

"Of course," Tyne said. "I need my chocolate."

"And he got tattoos on his face?" Ronnisha asked, thinking of the last two guys that Tyne had brought around – guys who had really been about that life for a little too long.

"Nope!" Tyne said, pointing her finger. "He don't got no tattoos on his face."

"Oh his neck count as the same thing too, girl," Ronnisha said, sensing something in Tyne's reaction.

"Oh," Tyne said, looking away. "Girl, why do all that matter? Anyway, like I was saying earlier before you wanted to be Ivanna and shit, he supposed to be comin' over tonight."

"You not gon' spend the night at his place?" Ronnisha asked.

"Naw," Tyne said. "He stay with his cousin. So, I told him that he could come to my place and stuff. Girl, I can't wait for him to come over. I know he got that good dick."

"Girl, I bet you do," Ronnisha said. "I know you. You always ask for the dick pic, first. Always."

"Girl, you got to," Tyne said. "A man can look at me," she pointed at her body, "and will already know what he gettin'. I feel like we should be able to do the same. I wanna know what he's packing and then I can really decide what I wanna do, or if I wanna do anything at all."

6

Ronnisha rolled her eyes as she stood up and set the blunt in the ash tray on the glass coffee table. She walked around the coffee table, over the bear-skin area rug, and over to the kitchen counter. She poured herself a glass of cranberry juice and noticed how the kitchen looked a little disorderly. "Damn," she said. "I forgot that I was supposed to clean all this up before Danez gets home."

"Oh, girl, stop with all that," Tyne said, standing up. "You so busy try'na be Miss Wifey for that nigga, but he ain't even put a ring on it."

"He got me livin' in this nice ass apartment, though," Ronnisha said. "What you got to say about that?"

Tyne hesitated. "I mean, girl, it's okay," she said, looking around. "Okay, this place is the shit. Danez still out in them streets doin' good, I see."

"Hmm, hmm," Ronnisha said. "He even got the barbershop and those couple stores over on the west side that be his front and stuff. He a smart ass nigga, I can tell you that."

"Well, girl, I'll get on home and stuff," Tyne said, grabbing her jacket. "I'm ready to get home and lay down for a minute and stuff. Work was tiresome today." Tyne worked at the front desk of a hotel downtown, not too far from where Ronnisha and Danez lived. Dressed in black dress pants and a cute, but professional, white top, she slid into her black collared jacket and grabbed her purse.

Ronnisha came over and hugged Tyne quickly. "Okay, I'mma get this place together before he get home and stuff," she said. "Let me know how tonight go, or if you survived, since you like them savages. Girl, I'mma be over here prayin' for you."

"Girl, boo," Tyne said, walking out the door. "Go ahead and clean up so that nigga you live with can give you some dick."

Ronnisha blushed as she closed the door, telling Tyne to go on somewhere. Once she was alone in her apartment once again, she quickly zipped around and picked up stray objects in efforts to straighten up the apartment. Just as she was washing the handful of dishes in the sink, she heard her cell phone vibrating from over on the couch. She dried her hands and rushed around to answer it. She smiled when she saw that it was Danez calling, loving how he always called to check on her.

"Hey," Ronnisha answered.

7

"Wassup, Baby?" Danez asked, his voice deep and raspy. "What you doin'?"

"Well," Ronnisha said, leaning over the counter that divided the dining area from the kitchen, "just straightening up a little bit. Actually, Tyne just left."

"Uh oh," Danez said then chuckled. "What she got goin'?"

"Some new nigga that she talkin' to now," Ronnisha answered, shaking her head. "You know how she is. I just sat there and listened and told her what I thought, as usual. He from Detroit, so at least she changed up her type a little bit."

"She ain't bringin' them niggas over to the place, is she, Ronnisha?" Danez asked. "You know how I feel about that."

"I know, I know," Ronnisha answered. "And no, you know I wouldn't let her do that and she would never do that. She was just on her way home from work, actually, and called to see what I was up to. She just came by to chat."

"Oh, okay," Danez said. "Well, I'm bout to stop and get us somethin' to eat and was just try'na make sure that you was home and shit before I did. I know what you like, so I'mma get it for you, okay? I'm going to Coritos."

Ronnisha's face lit up with excitement and she began to list off what she liked from the restaurant. Quickly, Danez cut her off by saying, "I told you, Baby. I know what you like. Just chill out. I'll be there in a little bit, so sit tight on that big ass booty."

"Nigga, stop with all that," Ronnisha said, blushing. "And my ass ain't that big."

"Shiiiiet," Danez said then chuckled. "A'ight then, I'mma be there in like thirty minutes, if that."

Ronnisha hung up and finished straightening up the apartment. About twenty five minutes passed before she heard keys jingling at the door. In came Danez, tall, brown-skinned, and handsome. He walked through the door, his muscles protruding through his white t-shirt. He slid out of his jacket, throwing it over the back of a chair in the dining area, then walked over to the kitchen. Glancing inside, he smiled at Ronnisha just as she was washing the last dish. Before she could say anything, Danez had rushed over and slid his hands around the small of her back. They then slid down and cupped her ass, slapping each cheek one at a time. They kissed.

8

"Hey, you," Ronnisha said.

"Wassup?" Danez said in return. His brown eyes were captivating to Ronnisha, as well as the fact that he was just a little under 6'3" and had a voice like the rapper Future. Ronnisha wondered if it was an Atlanta thing because up until Danez had turned 16 years old, he and his family lived in Atlanta. They'd only moved to Indianapolis when his stepfather had been offered a job at some big corporation downtown. "You ready to eat?" he asked Ronnisha. "I got your favorite in the bag in the dining room."

"Hell yeah," Ronnisha said.

Danez slapped her ass once again. "That's what I thought," he said. "Gotta keep this ass fat so it can keep takin' the dick good."

Ronnisha playfully pushed Danez away. The two of them walked into the dining area and sat down. As they ate their burritos, they talked about their days.

"Yeah, I put in some more applications today," Ronnisha said.

Danez looked at his woman with a face of contempt. "Why, Ronnisha?" he asked, in a very serious tone. "Why? I told you I got us. I got you, most importantly. You see all this?" He motioned, pointing around the apartment. "You see all this I got for us, not for me. I like you bein' here to hold a nigga down and stuff. And you know you ain't got to work. The shop and the stores are making money. Plus, me and Lamarcus and Marquis and Nieko is movin' work in these streets and shit like it ain't nothin'."

"I know," Ronnisha said, feeling a little guilty. "I know, I know, I know. But still, Danez. You know I need something to do all day and stuff. I mean, I appreciate the clothes." She thought about the numerous shopping sprees not only at malls in Indianapolis, but also at outlets in small towns outside of the city as well as the nice, big malls up in Chicago. "And the trips and stuff, but I do need something of my own."

"Okay," Danez said, holding his hands up. "Okay, I feel you. I guess I gotta respect that. At least you wanna do something for yourself."

"Exactly," Ronnisha said.

Ronnisha and Danez talked for a while about different things going on with Danez and his businesses, as he'd just come from his businesses. He was a little heated because he felt like one of his employees at the corner stores might be stealing from him. However, because a few importantly positioned cameras were broken, he couldn't prove it yet. Nonetheless, he considered himself to have had another good day, especially since he'd gone to see his boy Lamarcus and the two of them spent a considerable amount of time feeding dollar bills into a money counting machine in his basement. The smell of money was such a thrill to Danez, and he especially loved when there were more hundred dollar bills than he could ever imagine.

Danez and Ronnisha finished eating their burritos. As Ronnisha was gathering their trash up off of the table, Danez quickly stood up. He pressed his lips into the side of her neck and kissed her gently. Ronnisha turned and giggled. "Boy, what you doin'?" she asked.

No sooner than these words had spilled out of her lips, Ronnisha could feel Danez' manhood pushing against the back of her. Because he was wearing sweatpants, there was little in the way to keep her from feeling his meat.

"You know what I'm doin'," Danez said. "Don't try to play like you can't feel that dick pressing the back of you. I know you do."

"I do," Ronnisha said. "I do."

Danez pulled his head up to her ear and said, softly, "You know what I want. And you know you want it too."

Ronnisha turned around and squinted, looking into Danez's eyes. She then glanced down and grabbed his manhood, which was now rock hard and tenting in his sweatpants. Slowly and in a very sexual way, Ronnisha pushed Danez's chest back until he was sitting back in his chair. She then dropped to her knees and, with his assistance, slid his sweatpants down to his ankles. She then did the same with his black boxer briefs, freeing Danez's fat erection. Barely able to wrap her hand around the base, Ronnisha grabbed it and took it into her mouth. It didn't take Danez long to grip the dome of her head as his own head leaned back and he moaned.

"Fuck," Danez said. "Shit, you can suck dick. Fuck."

Danez, with a dizzy look on his face, licked and bit his lips as he looked down at Ronnisha. The sounds of her slurping on his manhood like a big, brown piece of chocolate filled the room. After about ten minutes, he couldn't take anymore. He reached down to help lift her up, having to practically pull Ronnisha's lips away from the head. "I want some of this pussy," he said. "You got the dick nice and wet for it."

Ronnisha never pushed back when Danez wanted to get into her panties. She prided herself in being the chick who had only slept with three guys in her life, and each of them were either relationships or long-term friends with benefits. Ronnisha stood up then slid her black leggings down, exposing her black panties. Danez pulled Ronnisha's shirt over her head then undid her bra. He smiled ear to ear when his eyes feasted on her big breasts hanging out and her nipples pointed in his direction. He leaned forward and pushed his face into her cleavage. The warmth on his cheeks caused his dick to get even harder. He leaned back into the chair a little bit and allowed Ronnisha to sit on it.

"Shit!" Ronnisha exclaimed, feeling the girth of Danez's manhood quickly fill her insides. Even though the two of them had been together for a couple of years, she still wasn't completely used to how Danez made her feel. Her eyes rolled back as she slid down on his manhood until all eight inches were inside of her. "Danez," she whimpered.

Danez chuckled, knowing how much chicks loved his dick. With a firm grip, he grabbed her waist and helped her to bounce up and down on his manhood. She screamed and squealed, not even caring if the neighbors heard, as Danez went from grabbing her waist to slapping her ass. Even from the front, Danez could see Ronnisha's ass cheeks bouncing around. Part of him was happy that they weren't doing it doggy style, as the sight of such a thing drove him crazy and would make him blow his load too soon.

Danez long stroked Ronnisha unmercifully until beads of sweat rolled down his face. Soon he let go inside of her. The soreness that Ronnisha now felt between her legs, as well as the aftershocks from the orgasm she'd gotten from the ten-minute quickie, left her unable to do anything but lean forward and fall into Danez's arms. He held her tightly as they calmed down. Their hearts beat in unison; they each breathed at a steady pace.

As the night sky darkened over the Indianapolis fall day, Danez and Ronnisha retired to their master bedroom. There, in their California king-sized bed, Danez held Ronnisha in his arms as they searched through Netflix for something to watch. They weren't

11

necessarily headed to bed, but they still enjoyed spending time relaxing with one another. It wasn't uncommon for Danez to have to go make money in the night, which didn't bother Ronnisha.

The two of them watched a couple of episodes of *The Walking Dead*, which Danez had turned on to scare the crap out of Ronnisha – something that always made her want to cling onto him even more, which he loved. Halfway through the second episode, Danez' phone rang.

"If you gotta go make that money, don't think you gotta sit around here with me," Ronnisha said, trying to be supportive. "For real, Danez."

"Hold up, hold up," Danez said, digging his phone out of his pocket. "Let's just see." He then saw that the person calling was his boy Lamarcus. Ronnisha instantly noticed the way his face scrunched up, almost looking as if he were confused as to why Lamarcus would be calling in the first place. "Wassup, nigga?" Danez answered.

Little did Danez know, his life was about to change. His boy Lamarcus was not calling about making any money. Rather, he was calling about a situation turned almost deadly – a situation that would send Danez into the streets of Indianapolis that night to help his friend; a situation that would only be the beginning of a new chapter not only for him and Lamarcus, but also for Ronnisha.

CHAPTER 2

"Shit this shit feel good!" Lamarcus exclaimed. Without leaning his head forward the least bit, he reached out and grabbed Rain's head. Even though she wasn't the prettiest chick in the hood or anything like that, her body was nice and petite. Her mouth game, however, and the fact that she had a pleasant attitude was especially appealing to Lamarcus. Not really the type to want to settle down, he was quickly considering. He had a nice time – literally – each and every time Rain would come by to kick it.

With Lamarcus' manhood filling Rain's mouth, all she could do was giggle. She didn't need Lamarcus' guidance to make her want to stay right where she was. As if her life depended on it, she continued bobbing her head up and down. She gave it all she had. It

12

was thrilling to hear Lamarcus, who she thought was incredibly sexy, moan so loudly.

"Suck that dick!" Lamarcus shouted. "This don't make no sense."

Lamarcus, who was about 5'10", thick build, and dark brown skinned lay back on his couch as Rain was on her knees, between his legs. He'd seen his buddy Danez out not too long ago. Soon after he left, he hit Rain up to see if she was free for the night. He was in luck because she was, as she'd broken up with her boyfriend about a month ago. Since then, Lamarcus had the chick over as often as he could, and let her stay for as long as she liked.

"I'm 'bout to bust," Lamarcus said. "Shit, don't stop. Don't stop."

Lamarcus squeezed so he could hold his load back, something he enjoyed doing to see how much pressure he could take and how long he could hold it back. Just as he was getting incredibly close to that feeling a man gets when he is about to let go, he heard something out in the front yard. Lamarcus had been living in his grandmother's house for the last six months – since she had been put into a nursing home. Her house was located in a neighborhood on the east side of the city, with a lot of wooded land surrounding it. Such an environment took Lamarcus a while to get used to.

"Shh," Lamarcus said, knowing that he needed to be aware of his surroundings. There was no doubt in his mind that he'd heard something outside. Reacting quickly, he jumped up. His manhood, which was still hard, caused Rain to gag and choke as she wasn't expecting him to get up unannounced.

Rain watched as Lamarcus pulled his white boxer briefs up and walked over to the window that looked out at the front yard. From the living room window, he could see most of the front yard except for the part that curved around the south end of the house. With squinting eyes, he looked through the blinds and scanned the yard, street, and yards across the street and even to the sides. His manhood had long gone down, as his heartbeat had sped up a little bit.

"What Lamarcus?" Rain asked, wiping slobber away from her mouth. "What is it? What's up? Is somebody supposed to be coming?"

"Shh," Lamarcus said, finding himself annoyed with Rain's country accent. "You see I'm try'na see what the fuck I heard."

"You just bein' paranoid and stuff, Lamarcus," Rain said, standing up. "I ain't hear nothin', so I don't know what you talkin' about."

I guess you wouldn't have, Lamarcus thought to himself then said, "Yeah. I heard something."

"It was probably some squirrel or some shit like that," Rain said. "You know you got all these woods around here. Why you trippin' over somethin' like that, especially if you don't see nothin'? For all you know, it coulda been one of those raccoons. You know more of them is comin' in the city and stuff. Is anybody out there?"

Lamarcus shook his head, regretting having ruined his orgasm because he thought he'd heard something. He and Rain had smoked some Kush before she got started making love orally to him. Lamarcus had always told himself he was going to stop smoking weed, but several failed attempts later, he still had not reached his goal.

"You right," he said, turning around and shaking his head. "I'm just trippin'."

Rain grabbed Lamarcus' meat through his boxer briefs. Lamarcus looked down and smiled, causing Rain to giggle with excitement. "That's okay, though," she said. "That just gimme the chance to suck on it longer."

"Yeah?" Lamarcus said, leaning forward. "You a freak?"

Rain remained silent as she turned around and walked back over to the couch. There, she dropped to her knees. Quickly, Lamarcus walked over and stood over her. No sooner than he'd pulled his underwear down to his ankles and stepped out of them, Rain, using only her mouth, had pulled his manhood back inside with her tongue. Lamarcus relaxed one again, with Rain grabbing his football player butt, as he grabbed her head and worked back up to her previous speed.

Again, Lamarcus heard noise outside. This time, it was talking. And this time, not only did he hear it, but Rain did as well. She pulled her head off of Lamarcus' dick and looked around. "Okay, I heard that," she said.

Just as Lamarcus was sliding his underwear back up over his tree trunk thighs, bullets flew into the house. The loud bangs of gunshots rang into the air, almost causing the house to rattle. Immediately, Lamarcus dropped down to the floor and pressed himself against the couch. Rain, screaming and not knowing what to do, got down as well. Lamarcus pulled her closer to him as the eighth, ninth, then tenth bullet came into the house. The living room window shattered, then did the patio door. Lamarcus heard the front door being blown open. This was almost like something out of a mafia movie. He felt as if he'd really had a hard look when he was standing at the window. If there was anybody out there, he would have been the person to see it. Nobody had better eyes than Lamarcus and he knew it.

With the gunshots still sounding off, Rain continued to scream as she feared for her life. Lamarcus struggled to think, but then remembered that he kept hit under the couch cushion, like any man would who did the kind of work he did. He knew that guys out in the streets could easily get jealous or what he and his boy Danez were doing for themselves. They were literally making money hand over fist – something that brings about envy even in the minds of people who have money.

Just as Lamarcus was reaching into the couch cushion, the gunshots stopped. Rain cried and pleaded, mumbling prayers that God would spare her from harm's way tonight. "Please, God. Please. Good God, please."

"Would you shut the fuck up?" Lamarcus said.

Just as Lamarcus was pulling his right arm out from under the couch cushion, he heard a footstep that sounded to be less than ten feet away. Quickly, he turned over. And there he looked into the eyes of someone he hadn't seen in a while, but had heard had beef with him. There stood, in the doorway between the family room and the living room, Qoree. He pointed a gun at Lamarcus and Rain, causing Rain to scream.

"Nigga, move your hand any more and I swear to God that you won't even fuckin' have one," Qoree said. Qoree, who was approaching 30 years old, stood at an even 6' height. His muscles made him all the more intimidating, as did the scar on the side of his face. With a stern look to his face, he was the kind of guy who could intimate the most street dudes while also turning their chicks on and making their panties wet. He'd had a problem with Lamarcus and Danez, as they were younger and tended to make moves in his hoods without asking him first. This was a hood felony in Qoree's eyes, and he wasn't afraid to let any dude in the streets figure that out. "Try me," he added.

Lamarcus froze.

"Lamarcus," Rain said. "Who is this crazy ass nigga? Who is this? Please don't kill me!"

Just then, three guys, dressed in black clothing just like Qoree, walked through the family room. Their feet crunched on the glass.

"Shut up," Lamarcus said. "Shut the fuck up, bitch." He then looked up to Qoree. "What the fuck you want, nigga?"

"Nigga, I'm the nigga with the gun," Qoree said, pointing his gun. "I ain't ask you to say shit so why the fuck is you talkin'? Nigga, you lucky I wasn't try'na kill you." He motioned his gun toward the shattered living room window. "Think of that as your fuckin' doorbell, nigga."

Qoree's three goons looked at one another and laughed. Qoree then told them to go over to the couch. "Stand them niggas up," he told them.

The three men rushed into the living room. One pulled Rain up off of the ground, taking his sweet time to look at her body. He snickered and nodded, then said, "Not too bad. This nigga might have a little taste."

The other two men pulled Lamarcus up. As much as he wanted to resist, and maybe go for his gun and hope that he'd loaded it before putting it under the couch cushion, he knew that any wrong move could turn out bad for him. With firm grips on both of his arms, he rose to his feet. Qoree looked at Lamarcus, looking him up and down. It was hard to miss the massive wet spot over his crotch, as well as the fact that the chick had slobber around her lips.

"I see I musta disturbed a little something," Qoree said. "My bad, nigga. Well, that's what the fuck happen when a nigga fuck around with me and don't show no respect. Look like she was suckin' your shit good, nigga!"

Lamarcus, furious to the core, looked down at the wet crotch of his boxer briefs. He then looked back up to Qoree and shook his head. "What the fuck you want, nigga?" he asked, feeling no fear in opening his mouth.

"I guess this nigga don't speak English no more," Qoree said. Quickly, he stepped forward and looked Lamarcus in the eye. After a long stare, he slapped him across the face. A groan slipped out of Lamarcus' mouth as the side of his face stung so bad. This, mixed with the fact that wind was starting to blow into the room and slam into his body, was almost unbearable. He held it together, though. No man could make him crumble. "What the fuck I say?" Qoree asked.

Qoree then stepped back and looked at the way Lamarcus had decorated his grandmother's house. "Damn, nigga," he said. "I heard this place was nice from some niggas I know that be goin' to the parties and shit you be havin', but I ain't know it was like this. Where the fuck you get this nice ass furniture from? I know them white people at the store was lookin' at you like I know this nigga doin' somethin' he ain't supposed to be doin' to be comin' in here and buyin' some shit like this. And damn nigga, you even got little statues and shit above the fireplace. Plants and shit. I see you and that other nigga makin' money."

Lamarcus pressed his lips together and nodded. Just then, Qoree slapped him across the face. This time, he went from the left to the right rather than the right to the left. "Nigga, I know you hear me talkin' to you," Qoree said.

Fuming, Lamarcus looked at Qoree. He had always thought that there would be that one nigga in this world that he would consider taking out. Qoree had just made that list and would, probably, stay at the top until the day one of them left this earth.

"What do you want?" Rain asked. "Please, just let me go. Let me go. I'm just a friend of his. I ain't got nothin' to do with what the fuck you got a problem with him for. I swear I don't. Why don't you just let me go?"

Qoree looked at Rain then Lamarcus. "I see why you keep this bitch on her knees," he said, boldly. "With how she talk, all it sound like she good for is suckin' dick. Fuck, that voice is annoying as fuck."

Rain was totally offended while also confused. She spoke softly. "Please," she said, just wanting to get out of there and never come back. "Please."

"Let her go, nigga," Lamarcus said. "She ain't got nothin' to do with this. She ain't even gotta be here."

"You right," Qoree said, nodding his head. "She should be outta this shit, shouldn't she?"

Just as Rain's hopes had brightened up, Qoree punched her across the face. With one blow, she was out cold. Her body had gone limp while in Qoree's goon's grasp. "Take this whinin' bitch in the other room and put her on the couch so we can talk about this money."

The man did as he was told. He picked Rain up and carried her into the other room. Quickly, he returned and stood behind Qoree.

"Where's the money you been takin' from me?" Qoree asked. "I want the fuckin' money."

"What money?" Lamarcus asked. "We ain't been takin' no money from you. This is money that we made that you ain't been try'na make."

Qoree laughed out loud then drove his fist into Lamarcus' stomach, causing him to lean over from the pain. "Nigga, maybe I should rephrase the question. I need my fuckin' money. How is that? I know you ain't keepin' the shit in no bank account and shit, is you? Y'all niggas gon' move into my hood and start makin' moves and shit, without talkin' to me first, but then think that I ain't gon' here about it. I know you had to have heard that a nigga run The Land. I know you have."

Lamarcus looked at Qoree then spit down toward the carpet. "Yeah," he said. "But he wasn't runnin' it real good if we can get in there and move work and shit. You know them niggas over there don't wanna work with your petty ass. You can't even do business. The only reason they do shit with your ass is 'cause you gotta scare niggas into wantin' to be bothered with you and shit. From what I hear, they prolly got a bullet out for your head right now."

Qoree was beginning to speak when he changed his course of thought. He pressed the barrel of his Saeilo gun into the temple of Lamarcus' head. Lamarcus tried to hide the fact that he was shaking, but doing so was incredible hard. "What?" he asked.

"The money," Qoree said. "Take me to the fuckin' money and all this can go away, nigga. It's really just that easy. Don't think for one minute that this shit it worth your life and shit, 'cause it's not, okay? You don't wanna send your mama to the grave and crying

18

and shit, dressed in all black, because her little boy was stupid and didn't do the right thing to not get his self killed."

Lamarcus hyperventilated. His nostrils were flared to the fullest as his chest pumped from breathing so hard. "Shit," he said. "I can't get the money if these two ugly ass goons you got is holdin' me in my place. You want the money or you want to stand here and just look at a nigga and shit?"

Qoree chuckled and made eye with all three of his goons in some unspoken code. "A'ight then, nigga," he said, directing his goons to let go of Lamarcus' arms. "Lead the way."

Lamarcus, free from the tight grip, walked ahead and toward the basement steps.

"Try some funny shit," Qoree said, "and I swear to God I will blow your head off and that dick suckin' bitch that's passed out in the other room. And let's make this quick. You look like you got white people that live around here, and you know how they are when it comes to callin' the police on niggas and shit."

Lamarcus led Qoree and his three dudes down into the basement. There, he walked across the entertaining area – a cluster of couches and chairs facing the television – and into a side room. Qoree told him to hold up, still not fully trusting that the man he was following wouldn't have at least a couple of tricks up his sleeves.

Qoree cautiously walked with Lamarcus into a side room where Lamarcus pulled a book case, which was positioned in a slanted way in the corner, out. Within seconds, a medium-sized metal safe was exposed. Qoree smiled and looked back at his boys, nodding.

"Open that shit," Qoree said. "Hurry up and open that shit, nigga. I heard y'all niggas be flashin' a lotta money and this is where I can find it. I wanna see what's in that safe and I want it all. Y'all not gon' move into my hood and start makin' money without talkin' to me first. You prolly the stupidest niggas that I ever fuckin' seen."

Reluctantly, Lamarcus leaned down and put the combination into the safe. He knew exactly how much money was in his possession – well into six figures – and he hated that his life depended on him coming off of it. Within thirty seconds or so, he had the safe door open. Just as he was reaching in, Qoree pulled him back by his arm. "Watch out, nigga," he said.

Qoree looked into the safe and pulled out the money machine. Just behind it were stacks upon stacks of bundled money. He licked his lips, almost happy that these couple of younger dudes had come into his hood. In many ways, this was easy money.

"You got a duffle bag or some shit, nigga?" Qoree asked Lamarcus.

Without speaking, Lamarcus stood up and pulled a black bag that he'd used to go out of town from the other side of a spare twin bed. He handed it to Qoree, almost have to catch himself as he felt himself starting to throw the bag at him.

"Nigga, you not gettin no attitude, is you?" Qoree asked.

Lamarcus simply shook his head. He stood there and watched as Qoree told his goons to come over and empty the money into the safe. Obediently and with weak minds, they did just as they were told. Thousands upon thousands of dollars that he and his boy Danez had worked for slowly emptied into the black bag and walked out the door.

Qoree, keeping his gun firm, walked Lamarcus back upstairs. Once they'd gotten back to the living room, Qoree knew it was time to really teach Lamarcus a lesson. Taking the money wasn't enough, as some dudes in the streets needed physical reminders of how things were supposed to work.

Qoree backed away, grabbing the heavy bag of money. He looked at his three goons and pointed at Lamarcus. Just then, Lamarcus' heart jumped. He felt like an animal trapped in a corner. Three dudes, who were all bigger than him, even if only in height, surrounded him. Immediately, he began swinging but his efforts were just that: efforts. It only took a matter of seconds for him to lose his balance in the mists of six separate fists swinging at his head. He stumbled down to the floor, still putting up a fight because that was just the kind of man he'd always been.

"That's right, nigga," Qoree said, watching Lamarcus' face slowly become more and more bruised – noticing how his punches were getting slower. "Fuck this nigga up. Don't let me catch you or that bitch ass nigga you cool with doin' shit else over in The Land, okay? You understand me, nigga? This ain't no shit to play with 'cause you playin' with my money. You playin' with my money, nigga."

Now, Qoree's goons were kicking Lamarcus all over his body. There were blood stains on the carpet from where he'd coughed up blood. Tears rolled down his eyes as he'd never taken such a rough beating. In so many ways, he wanted to just die. The only bright side was the fact that it wasn't taking place out in the street and for others to see and possibly capture on their phones.

"Stand this nigga up," Qoree ordered, feeling a sense of urgency at this point.

The three goons lifted Lamarcus up, having to hold him up to keep him from falling back to the floor. There were bruises and scrapes all over his body. Both eyes were blackened and nearly swollen shut. Not to mention both of his lips were busted and bleeding profusely.

Qoree, wanting to get his own licks in before they left, looked around. He noticed that there was an additional room on the other side of the kitchen. From where they stood, he could see that there was a pool table. He ordered his goons to carry Lamarcus into the room. Dragging him by his feet, they did just that and, under Qoree's guidance, lifted his weak and limp body up onto the pool table. Qoree grabbed a pool stick and began to lash Lamarcus over the back, causing him to yell from the pain and beg Qoree to stop.

Qoree, now laughing uncontrollably, lashed Lamarcus over the back one last time – one last time with so much force that the pool stick broke in half. He dropped the half that he'd been holding and leaned over, looking into Lamarcus' face. "Nigga, make me come back," he said. "Do some more shit and make me come back."

Having proven his point, Qoree motioned to his goons that it was time to leave. The three men followed their leader out of the front door, the last in line turning the lights out in each room. Still conscious, Lamarcus noticed, even through his swollen eyes, that his house had gone dark. He really couldn't see much, except for the silhouettes of different pieces of furniture. And that was only because light shined into the house from the streetlight out in front of the front yard.

"Fuck," Lamarcus mumbled, barely able to open his mouth. Every part of his body throbbed. He felt like he was slowly dying because the pain was so great. His blood boiled with anger as he knew that if he survived tonight, he would get revenge in the sweetest way possible.   Lamarcus managed to lift his leg after

21

ten minutes or so. He was surprised that he didn't hear any sirens yet. His neighbors, which were spread out, could have very well not have been home. On top of that, a few houses were empty as well. Moving very slowly, he slid himself off of the pool table and down onto the floor. He was so numb he nearly didn't feel his body hitting the floor, but he knew it when he was looking eye level with the bottoms of vases.

Crawling, Lamarcus made his way back into the living room. He felt so weak. His breathing was slow. He managed to pull himself up to his couch and reach up to grab his phone. With one eye just barely opening a fraction of an inch, Lamarcus looked into his text log and tapped Lamarcus' name. He listened as the phone rang, mumbling, "Answer the phone, nigga." He took a deep breath, trying to stay conscious. "Answer the phone."

CHAPTER 3

As soon as Danez got off the phone with Lamarcus, he jumped back into his clothes. As he rushed, he explained to Ronnisha what was going on – that Lamarcus had been attacked and beaten by Qoree and his boys. Ronnisha, like any local chick would, took the time to ask who Qoree was. Before blazing out of the door, Danez said, "This nigga that think he own The Land. I told you about that nigga last week."

"The one who came in the store try'na ask questions and shit?" Ronnisha asked, for clarification. She shook her head.

"Yeah," Danez said.

"Yeah, I know that nigga," Ronnisha said. "Well, I don't really know him, know him like that, but I heard about it and seen him around, especially when I be down in the hood. I'm surprised y'all ain't cross paths."

"Shit, I though the nigga went back down south somewhere with how them niggas over on the west side be talkin' about his ass," Danez said, sliding into his shoes. "They talk about him like the nigga got ran out."

"Do you want me to go?" Ronnisha asked. "I mean, if Lamarcus really got beat up that bad, maybe I should go and help you."

Danez paused for a moment to think about it. If he were sure that Lamarcus was alone in his house, and not with some chicks, he wouldn't have had a problem with her going. However, Danez knew his boy Lamarcus and knew that there was rarely a night where he didn't have a female over. And there had even been times that they'd pass a female around – times that he wanted to make sure Ronnisha never learned about.

"Naw, that's all right," Danez said. "I mean, I don't know how bad it is. He was sayin' something about the house got all shot up and shit. And the nigga was mumbling. I'll let you know what hospital we go to and you can come down there if you want. Let me go and see how bad this shit is."

Quickly, Danez kissed Ronnisha and rushed out the door. He rolled the elevator down to the garage floor of the apartment building and hurried into his white 2014 Ford Explorer. Danez hurried out of that garage and up onto New York Street. From there, he headed right through the northern half of downtown Indianapolis

23

and made his way east. As the condos and office buildings of downtown passed him by, either side of the streets slowly changing to brick apartment buildings then houses, Danez struggled with watching his speed. He'd never heard of Lamarcus getting beat the way he made it sound over the phone. Danez literally shook his head as he remembered the way his boy was mumbling. It was almost hard to make out what he was saying.

Danez turned down Hawthorne Lane, on the city's east side. The street was lined with nice, ranch-style homes. Large front yards were rather wooded, making the street even darker. The houses seemed to hide behind the forestry. After a couple of blocks, the properties came to be further and further apart. Soon enough, Danez had pulled up in front of where Lamarcus stayed. While the house was indeed dark, he could see a little too much detail of the curtains and inside of the house from the street. It was very clear that several of the front windows had been blown out. Much of the block was dark, leaving Danez to wonder if neighbors were at home or if somebody had called the police and they simply didn't know where to go. If he were just riding by, he probably wouldn't notice anything out of the ordinary. The front yard was so wooded that a person would have to take the time to stop and look between the trees.

Danez turned into the driveway and rolled up to the side of the house. When he parked his SUV and got out, he could hear Lamarcus' cries for help. "In here," he said. "In here."

Danez looked over a window seal and saw the glass shattered on the carpet. He then saw Lamarcus, who looked as if he were just a few punches from seeing the light and passing on to the afterlife.

"Shit," Danez said. "I'm coming, man. I'm coming."

Danez went around the house until he came to the front door. It was pulled closed, or so it seemed as he walked up. Upon stepping closer, he saw that it was open. He rushed into the house. The first thing to greet him was a passed out chick on the couch. She was dressed in nothing but her bra and panties. Immediately, Danez reach down and shook her. Frightened, she woke up and looked into Danez's eyes. Just then, Danez realized that he was looking at Rain, a chick that Lamarcus had been talking to and getting somewhat serious about.

"Rain?" Danez said. "Calm down, okay? Calm down. It's Danez."

Quickly, Rain calmed down and lifted herself up upright on the couch. "Oh my God," she said, putting her hand over your mouth. Her head turned and she looked into the other room. "Oh no, Danez." She began to cry and sob as she thought about what might have happened.

Rain tried to get up, but she quickly lost her balance. She grabbed her head as she tried to walk forward, only falling back into the couch.

"Wait right there," Danez said. "You can't do it right now. Just wait right there."

Danez moved forward into the house until he came into the living room. There, he found Lamarcus on the floor, in nothing but his boxer briefs. He was trying to crawl toward the doorway, but looked to be having the hardest time in the world. His body was bruised all over. Blood was everywhere, as Danez could see the trail leading back into the room with the pool table. Even in the dimly lit room, he saw the broken pool stick. With that, he was able to put two and two together and figure out some of what happened.

Danez rushed over to Lamarcus and knelt down. "Damn, nigga," he said, feeling his heart sink. "What the fuck happened?"

Danez helped Lamarcus to turn over and lie on his back. He looked into his face – swollen eyes, so much so that they were shut, busted lip, scratches and bruises on his face.

Lamarcus tried to explain but was clearly unable to talk. When his lips had barely opened, Danez could see that a couple of his teeth had been knocked out as well.

"Come on, man," Danez said. "I know this is gon' hurt, but we gotta get you to the hospital, man. You could die and shit."

"Nigga, no I ain't," Lamarcus said, proudly. "Don't take me to no hospital. You know them niggas work at the hospital and shit and they get to talkin'. Don't take me to no hospital."

Danez looked at Lamarcus and shook his head. "Naw, man," he said. "Fuck all that. Dude, you should see what you look like. We gotta get you to the hospital."

Quickly, Danez went and opened the back door, as it was closer to the driveway at the side of the house. When he returned, he lifted Lamarcus up and eventually, with the help of swinging his arms over his shoulder, got him to stand. He looked at Lamarcus' face, never having seen someone so badly beaten. Qoree and his boys showed no mercy on his best friend. Danez then felt guilt come over him, as he knew that the aggression Lamarcus had just received was also directed at him. It was uncomfortable, to say the least, to think about how that could have been him at his apartment downtown. Furthermore, instead of Rain being knocked unconscious and left on a couch in her bra and panties, it very well could have been Ronnisha. Right then and there, Danez made a mental note to call Ronnisha when they got to the hospital and tell her that she needed to go stay somewhere else for the night. For all Danez knew, Qoree and his goons could be headed downtown after leaving Lamarcus' house.

"Man, you not gon' take me…you not gon' take me in just my drawers, is you?" Lamarcus asked, struggling to get the words out. "Man, don't do that to me…" His words were trailing off. Any thought of putting his pants on had slipped Danez' mind. There was so much blood and it dripped everywhere.

"Come on, nigga," Danez said. "Come on."

Danez walked Lamarcus' nearly lifeless body out to his SUV and helped to lay him across the backseat. He then rushed back into the house to see what was going on with Rain. When he got to the front room, he found that she had slid into some pants and was already sliding into a shirt.

"Come on," Danez said. "I'm 'bout to take him to the hospital. Come on."

With a sense of urgency, Rain rushed out behind Danez. They closed the door to the house then jumped into the SUV. Carefully, Danez backed out of the driveway and made his way toward the highway. Driving as fast as he could without getting pulled over, he headed toward the interstate so he could get to the closest hospital.

Danez looked back at Lamarcus every so often as he drove down the interstate. "Shit, shit, shit," he said. "What the fuck happened? What the fuck happened to that nigga?"

"I don't know," Rain said, crying and shaking her head. "I just don't know. I don't know, I don't know. We were there, chilling and stuff, you know, and then Lamarcus said he heard somethin' outside. We both thought he was just trippin'. Right when we calmed down, though, they started shooting up the house." Rain had

26

to calm herself down from thinking about the horrible experience. "I was so scared. I swear, Danez, I thought I was gon' die."

Danez nodded. "Fuck that nigga Qoree," he said.

"Why did he do this?" Rain asked. "Why he come up in there and do all that? What the fuck is going on?"

"It's complicated," Danez said, not wanting to talk too much. While he was well aware that Lamarcus was beginning to catch feelings for Rain, he still didn't know exactly how far those feelings went. In light of that, he didn't want to talk too much and have her know things that she simply didn't need to know.

"The money," Lamarcus murmured from the backseat. "The money."

"What he sayin'?" Danez asked. He tried to look back but the interstate was too busy. "What he sayin', Rain? What he sayin'?"

Rain leaned toward the back. "Something about money," she said, leaning back into the front.

"Money?" Danez asked, trying to make sense of that one word coming out of his boy's mouth. He then realized what he was saying. "Fuck!" he exclaimed.

"What, Danez?" Rain asked. "What? What is it?"

Danez looked over at Rain. "That nigga Qoree and his boys got the money. That's what they came there for. To get the money. Fuck, I knew them niggas over in The Land couldn't be trusted. And I told that nigga Lamarcus about havin' them over for parties and shit. That's probably the way they found out where he lived."

Rain looked out the window, at the interstate, remaining silent – a silence that would not go unheard by Danez.

As Danez got off of the interstate and drove down 16th Street to get to the hospital, he kept telling Lamarcus to just hold on. "Don't you die on me, nigga," he said. "Don't you fuckin' die on me. We gon' get these niggas for doin' this shit. And we gon' get our money, too. He not gon' run us up out The Land when them niggas who live over there don't even want the nigga round, either."

Rain looked over at Danez, wishing that she could fill some of the missing puzzle pieces. However, Lamarcus' health was far more important at the moment. Within a few minutes, Danez was pulling his SUV out in front of the Emergency Room doors. He quickly jumped out of the car and got the attention of the hospital staff just inside. They quickly came rushing out and Danez opened the door, showing Lamarcus to them.

"Oh my Lord," a middle-aged white man said upon leaning into the SUV. "What the hell happened to this young man?"

"Can you help him?" Danez asked, in a snappy way. "Damn, can you help him so he don't die?"

"Yes, of course," the man said. He motioned for the hospital staff to bring out a stretcher. The man, with the assistance of three female staff members, lifted Lamarcus on to the stretcher and rolled into the hospital. Danez followed them inside, as the staff opened Lamarcus' eyes and looked at his pupils. "This isn't good," the man said. "This is not good."

"Y'all can't let him die," Danez said as they got onto the elevator. They headed up to the 2nd floor. "Y'all betta not let my nigga die like that. Ain't like he shot or nothin'."

"Calm down," the man said. "And sometimes other physical injuries can be worse than bullets. Please, just let us do our jobs, okay? Just let us do our jobs."

They got off of the elevator and headed into the emergency operating room. Here, Danez was pushed out into the hallway. Feeling anxious, and in many ways afraid for his own safety, he looked around at every doorway and window in the hospital. He then pulled his phone out to call Ronnisha. He shook his head as he held the phone up to the side of his face, hoping to God that Ronnisha hadn't fallen asleep. There was just no telling what Qoree and his boys would do next, if anything at all.

"You not sleep, are you?" Danez asked.

"Naw," Ronnisha said. "I mean, you just left a little bit ago. Shit, I'm sittin' up here with my clothes on and stuff so I can be ready to come down to the hospital. What happened to Lamarcus? Is he gon' be okay? Are you at the hospital yet? Which one so I can get in the car and come on down there?"

"Naw, naw, Ronnisha," Danez said. "And it ain't good. When I got there, I found him on the floor and they beat his ass pretty bad. Like the nigga was damn near unconscious and shit. I mean, I ain't never seen no shit like it. All this blood everywhere. Bruises all over his back. Both his lips busted. His face all sorts of fucked up. His eyes so black that they swollen shut. I could barely see him open them."

28

"Oh no," Ronnisha said, in a very caring way. "That is horrible."

"Exactly," Danez said, thinking about Ronnisha's safety. "That's why I need you to go stay somewhere else tonight. I know, I know, it's not what you was thinkin', and I might be over reactin', but I don't know what the fuck that nigga Qoree is gon' do next. I doubt he know where we stay, but you never know."

"Of course," Ronnisha said. She could hear the anguish in her man's voice. The last thing she'd want to do was make his feelings any worse. "I can call Tyne and see what she doin'. You know that's my best friend. She gon' let me come and stay over, probably."

"Okay," Danez said. He then looked around the waiting room, noticing that other people were sitting around. He saw a corner on the other side that had fewer people. And the people who were sitting there were rather spread out. Danez quickly hurried over to that area and spoke quietly into the phone. "And Baby, listen," he said. "Get that semiautomatic handgun we keep in the bathroom."

"Okay," Ronnisha said, in a very serious tone.

"You remember when I took you to the range and shit and showed you how to use it, right?" Danez asked. "You think you can handle yourself with that? I just want you to carry it so you can watch your back and shit and not be totally unprepared."

"Yeah, I can handle it," Ronnisha said. "I wish a nigga would try to walk up on me."

"Yeah, well, just be watchin' your back and shit in the parking garage," Danez said. "You never know when some nigga might have got in through the door or something. And you know that man who work at night downstairs be fallin' asleep and stuff, so really watch out."

"Okay," Ronnisha said. "I'm 'bout to get it, hit Tyne up, and be on my way out the door."

"Okay, I love you," Danez said. "Let me know when you on your way to Tyne and when you get there. Remember what I told you about them niggas that she be hangin' around. Watch them too."

"Okay, love you too," Ronnisha said, ending the call.

Danez pushed his phone back into his pocket and headed back toward the hallway. Just as the doctor—an older black woman who looked similar to the actress Angela Basset – approached.

Behind her was two police officers. "Fuck," Danez said, the words slipping out of his mouth. He hadn't seen the black doctor when they were pushing Lamarcus to the back. However, now all he could see was white. There was no way in hell he wanted to talk to two police officers, especially considering the life he lived. He was able to rest assured in the fact that he'd stayed under the radar thanks to the stores and barbershop he had on the west side—businesses he'd worked hard to build, and used well to stay out of the light out in the streets.

"Hello, young man," the doctor said. "These two police officers would like to talk to you quickly about what happened to your friend. I hope you don't mind, but the hospital takes the liberty of calling the police when the patient is in a really bad state."

"Oh, okay," Danez said, trying to put on his nice voice.

The doctor walked away, leaving Danez with the two officers. Both had stern white faces and military-like buzz cuts. They stepped forward. One, whose name was Officer Morgan, appeared to be the leader as he did most of the talking.

"So, buddy," he said. "Tell us about what happened to your friend."

Danez was very careful with what he said during his explanation. Furthermore, he made sure to leave Qoree's name out of it. He could only imagine the destruction and carnage that would take place in the hood if he were found to be the reason for the police cracking down on anybody, let alone Qoree. People in the streets may have hated his guts, or so they said, but they knew better than to make him mad because of his reach from having such deep roots in The Land.

Danez's story included him getting a call from Lamarcus to come over, which they usually did at night anyway. When he got there, he found the house shot up and Lamarcus and the young lady – Rain – who was now downstairs being treated for minor injuries, in their current states. Reluctantly, and really seeing no way out of it, Danez gave up Lamarcus' address to the police. He could only hope that there was nothing incriminating. He felt pretty confident in the fact that there wouldn't be, as Lamarcus was pretty good about keeping his stuff tight and together.

The police officers' took Danez' statement, which they each found to be interesting as the point of view was so limited. When

30

they walked away, they looked back at Danez and looked him up and down. The leading officer, Morgan, then said, "We'll get some officers over to the house so we can figure out who did this to your buddy, man. Just remember," he paused and made purposeful, distinct eye contact with Danez, "if you know anything you're not telling us, you could get into trouble."

"I've told you everything I know," Danez said. "But if I find anything else out, I'mma call y'all, okay? I wanna find who did this too."

The officers disappeared onto the elevators. Danez, now sitting in the waiting room, looked at his phone. He debated about calling Lamarcus' mother, who had basically been like an aunt to him since he and Lamarcus were friends. If he hadn't been waiting so long to hear back from Ronnisha, his thoughts might have gone elsewhere. He hoped and prayed that Ronnisha didn't have any problems. If Danez had known that the beating was this bad, and that the house would be shot up like in the gang movies set out in Los Angeles with drive-by shootings, he would have brought Ronnisha with him. If nothing else, he could at least be sure that she was safe. The idea of her making moves out in the streets at night, with a gun she may or may not remember how to use, did not sit well with him.

Finally, Danez decided to go ahead and call Lamarcus' mother, Amber. He would feel too guilty with himself if he didn't let her know what was happening. As the phone rang, and he waited on her to answer, he tried to think of how he would tell her that her son had almost been beaten to death. What made matters worse was the fact that Lamarcus had done such a good job keeping his street life away from his mother. However, she was a smart woman; there was no doubt that she probably picked up on it. With her being what many would call a young, hot mama, she was probably using some of the money that her son made to go shopping. She was always dressed in the hottest clothing. And even though she was coming up on being 40 years old, she still was confident in knowing that she could compete with the young girls in high school who really thought they had something going on for themselves.

"Hello?" Amber answered.

"Miss Amber?" Danez said. "It's Danez. How you doing?"

"Oh, hay, Danez," Amber said, clearly sounding as if she were caught off guard. "I'm okay, I guess. How are you?"

"Well," Danez said, hesitantly. "I could be better. Are you at home right now?"

"Yes I am," Amber answered. "Danez, Baby, what's goin' on? Why are you calling me this late at night, especially on a weekday? What's wrong? What happened?" She gasped. "Ain't nothin' happen with Lamarcus, did it? Danez, tell me that ain't nothin' happened to my baby."

"We at the hospital, Miss Amber," Danez said. "Earlier, Lamarcus called me. These niggas ran up in his house and jumped on him."

"Ran up in his house?" Amber asked. "In my mama's house?"

"Yeah," Danez asked. "They shot the place up, but Lamarcus wasn't shot, so don't worry about that. They just….they just beat him up pretty bad. Miss Amber, I got him to the hospital as soon as I could."

At Miss Amber's request, Danez explained the state in which he'd found Lamarcus. These details were all Amber needed to hear. She was soon on her way. No sooner than Danez had gotten off of the phone with his best friend's mother, his phone vibrated. It was a text message from Ronnisha, saying that she was at Tyne's house.

The next several minutes seemed twice as long as Danez waited in the hospital waiting room. He thought about what his next move could be.

CHAPTER 4

Ronnisha made it down to the parking garage and into her red 2013 Honda Accord without any problem. She walked cautiously, always looking around a corner before she walked out into the hallway. When she'd gotten down into the garage, she made sure to take a moment to look through the cars and see if she saw the tops of any heads. She then even went as far as kneeling down to the ground and looking under the cars. Once she realized that she was the only breathing soul in the garage, she rushed out to her car and drove off.

Once she pulled out into the streets of downtown Indianapolis, she called her girl Tyne. She was in luck, as she answered and sounded as if she was not anywhere close to going to sleep.

"Tyne, girl, what you doin'?" Ronnisha asked. "I need a favor."

"Girl, just got done with that nigga," Tyne said, confidently. She then put on her sleepy voice. "Girl, he fucked me so good."

"Girl, you nasty," Ronnisha said. "Please, please, please tell me you not talkin' like this in front of him and stuff while I'm on the phone with you."

"Naw, girl," Tyne said. "I ain't. I got up when I saw you callin'. I'm out in my livin' room. What's up? Are you drivin'? Girl, where you and Danez headin'?"

"That's the thing," Ronnisha explained. "Somethin' done happened. I need to come over to your place tonight 'cause it ain't safe to go back to our apartment. Or, at least, that's what Danez is saying."

"Girl, are you serious?" Tyne asked. "Oh my God, girl, what happened? Okay, okay. You can come on over. I'mma have the door unlocked. I need to hear about this 'cause I can hear it all in your voice that you runnin' scared and worried. Girl, hurry up and get over here."

Tyne lived in an apartment complex out on Post Road, which was one of Indianapolis' roughest parts of town. What made the area different though is that it was not anywhere close to downtown. Rather, it was on the far-east side of the city. Ronnisha took Interstate 70 out east and got off at Post Road then headed north. Post Road was a wide street with rundown apartment complexes on either side. The intersections were wide open with drugstores and liquor stores booming, even in the middle of the night.

Ronnisha pulled into the parking lot and headed upstairs. Just as she was reaching for Tyne's doorknob, the door swung open. She quickly stepped inside and immediately smelled burning incense. She hugged Tyne, who looked worried, dressed in her pajamas and red robe.

"Girl, come in," Tyne said. "Come in, come in, come in."

"Girl, calm down," Ronnisha said, snickering. "This ain't no damn James Bond movie or nothin' like that."

"Well, you the one rushin' over here in the middle of the night, Ronnisha," Tyne said. "Obviously somethin' serious done happened or else you wouldn't be here."

Just as Ronnisha was sliding out of her jacket, she noticed a pair of men's tennis shoes by the door. She looked down at them then up at Tyne. She smiled. "Girl, don't tell me you still got that nigga Shannon over here while I'm here."

"Well, what did you want me to do?" Tyne asked. "I mean, did you want me to just kick him out of bed. I woke him up and told him that you'd be coming over, so you ain't got to worry about him walkin' around naked in the middle of the night or nothin' like that. Girl, after the dick down he gave me, he need to sleep for the rest of the night. I'm just sayin." She raised her hands up toward the ceiling as if she were celebrating in church. "So, girl, what the hell happened?" She looked Ronnisha up and down, noticing that she clearly wasn't dressed as flashy as she would normally be dressed.

Ronnisha sat down on Tyne's couch, sent a text to Danez saying that she'd made it safely, and explained. The two talked back and forth about it for the rest of the night, each offering her point of view on who was involved and why. Both of them had heard of Qoree, but didn't really know much about him. By about one o'clock, they were tired. Ronnisha went to sleep on the couch and Tyne went back into the bedroom, happily lying down next to her newest love interest.

Ronnisha woke up in the morning hearing something move around. It sounded as if it were coming from Tyne's bedroom. She looked over that way, moving the blanket away from her face. There was indeed a light on, shining under the door. Within a matter of minutes, the door opened. Ronnisha pushed her face back down into the pillows, pulling the blanket up over her face. She watched as the Shannon guy, who was tall, with light skin and a freckled face, walked out of the bedroom. Tyne followed closely behind, glowing like a woman does after good sex the night before. She whispered a few things to him, one of which was about his manhood, before he left, saying something about having to get to work.

Ronnisha watched as Tyne closed the door, pulling her head back in from watching Shannon head back out to the apartment complex parking lot. When Tyne turned around, Ronnisha opened her eyes wide. This caught Tyne's attention, as she could see white in Ronnisha's face in the dimly lit room. Tyne, as nosey as she wanted to be, stepped forward and looked down into Ronnisha's face. She had always wanted to see a person who slept with their eyes open.

"Girl, I know you see me lookin' at you," Ronnisha said in a very flat voice.

Tyne jumped back, a little scared. Ronnisha leaned upright on the couch and shook her head. "Girl, you nasty," she said as she stood up and stretched. "I heard what you said to that nigga when you walked him to the door like you his wife or somethin'.."

"Girl, you ain't hear nothin'," Tyne said, sashaying away and toward her kitchen. "Anyway, how long was you sittin' up watchin' and stuff and not gon' even say good morning or nothin' like that?"

"I mean," Ronnisha said, "it wasn't like I was watchin' all that closely. I just heard y'all movin' around and stuff then the door opened. He's cute, though. Don't even really look like he from Detroit."

"Girl, you betta stop throwin' shade at Detroit," Tyne said. "Anyway," her voice changed to a more serious tone, "have you heard from Danez about Lamarcus or not?"

Ronnisha picked her phone up off of the floor. She shook her head. "Naw," she said. "I mean, he was probably at the hospital all night. I ain't wanna bother him or nothin' like that."

"Girl, I feel you on that," Tyne said. She opened her refrigerator to see what she had to eat. Her pickings looked slim. "Shit," she said. "My cousin still ain't hit me up with them food stamps yet. She be flakey as shit."

"Tyne, you wasn't gon' cook nothin', was you?" Ronnisha asked. Her tone was very sarcastic. "We can just skip that and go get

35

us some McDonalds or somethin' like that. I mean, you know you can't really cook. Remember that French toast you made? We all was in here choking from how thick that shit was."

Tyne looked out into the living room at her girl Ronnisha and shook her head. "Say something else like that," she said, pointing her finger, "and we gon' fight."

The two women spent the next several minutes getting ready. By 8 o'clock, they were headed out the door. Tyne insisted on driving, so Ronnisha climbed into the passenger side seat of her gold-colored Camry.

"So," Tyne said, "what do you think that Danez is gon' do? He not just gon' let this stuff get worse and worse until it all really blow up, is he?"

"I don't know, yet," Ronnisha said. "But, Tyne, you gotta promise me that you not gon' say nothin'. You know you like a sister to me, for real, for real. And you know that Danez like you, but…"

"He feel like I'mma say somethin' or somethin'?" Tyne asked.

"Well, not exactly that either," Ronnisha said, trying to be cautious about how she approached the topic. "If you want the truth, the truth is that Danez ain't so much worried about you and your mouth, but he worried about them niggas you bring around."

"What?" Tyne asked, feeling a little offended. "Damn, you ain't have to just make me sound like a hoe."

"Girl, I ain't sayin' that you no hoe or nothin' like that," Ronnisha said. "I'm just tellin' you. And girl, I swear to God, you betta not go talkin' about this shit to nobody. And I mean to nobody."

"Girl, I ain't, I ain't," Tyne said.

"Hmm, hmm," Ronnisha said. "But, anyway, I had been talkin' to Danez about me goin' out and gettin' a job, so he must be out here makin' some real money. He don't want me to work, even though I used to, you know, when we first started talkin' and stuff. Ever since I lost that last job, he been on his grind so hard and he just want me to sit home and chill."

"So, girl, why you complainin'?" Tyne asked. "Shit, I wish I had a man I could point at stuff and he just buy it for me. You got the life everybody else want."

36

"Yeah, right," Ronnisha said.

Tyne glanced over at Ronnisha. "I know what it is," she said, reading her friend's face. "You worried about where some of that money came from?"

"I mean…" Ronnisha began, hesitating. "I mean, basically, yeah. I can tell that he really out here makin' a lot of money and I just ain't know he was movin' work like that."

"Well, you know what them niggas out in the streets say," Tyne said, rolling her eyes. "Indiana is the Crossroads of America, so they got a lot of shit movin' through here. Hold up…" She paused to think. "You don't think that he movin' that stuff that them white folks is pickin' back up again?"

"What you talkin' about?" Ronnisha asked.

"That heroine shit or whatever they call it," Tyne asked.

Ronnisha immediately began shaking her head. "Naw," she said. "Nope. I know Danez, girl, and trust me, he ain't movin' no shit like that. He betta than that. All it take is for one of these white cops to get his ass and them racist ass white people downtown gon' throw him under the jail."

"I know," Tyne said. "That's just what I was thinking."

Tyne rolled up to the McDonalds drive-thru lane. Because it was morning rush hour, the line was backed up. Since this was a well-run location, however, the line quickly moved ahead. Ronnisha noticed Tyne was still silent. "Girl, you really don't think that Danez is involved in that kind of stuff, do you?"

Tyne shrugged her shoulders as she looked over at Ronnisha. "Girl, if you don't think he is, then who am I to say otherwise?" she asked, rhetorically. "I was just asking you a question is all."

Ronnisha nodded. They waited until they pulled up and ordered their food. When the Hispanic workers in the window handed the bags into the car, Tyne pulled off and headed back toward the apartment complex. She and Ronnisha chatted most of the way, mainly about how Tyne felt about Shannon and how Ronnisha felt about what was going on with Danez and Lamarcus.

"Girl, maybe later on, we can find out where Lamarcus is and go see him," Tyne suggested. "I mean, I know he's Danez's boy and stuff, but we was cool and stuff too. I remember when y'all had that get together for his birthday. That shit was fun."

"Yeah, it was," Ronnisha said, deep in thought.

Tyne pulled back into her parking spot out in front of her apartment building. Just as she and Ronnisha were climbing out of the car with their McDonald's bags, Tyne stopped and looked down the sidewalk. Instantly, Ronnisha noticed Tyne was looking at a chick coming out of the next doorway. "Girl, what?" Ronnisha asked.

"There that bitch go," Tyne said, shaking her head as she continued getting out of the car. "She betta not bring her ass down here or she just might get jumped on."

"What she do to you?" Ronnisha asked.

"Remember when I told you when I first met Shannon and shit?" she asked. "And I told you about that chick that live in my complex that was all up in his face one day when he was standin' out by his car and just waitin' on me to come down?"

"Girl, yes," Ronnisha said, looking back down at the chick. She was now much closer, maybe three or four parking spaces away. "Ole disrespectful bitch."

"Exactly," Tyne said.

The chick – Neeci – came walking by. At only 5'1" in height, she had some of the biggest lips around. In fact, her lips were the very thing that got her so much attention. She'd only lived in the King James Apartments for six months and she already had a reputation for going down on every dude with swag and a nice car. Once word had gotten around, she quickly made enemies with numerous females in the complex, particularly if they had men around. This chick showed no shame in showing any attention to someone else's man, even if that other chick was standing right there and looking dead into her face.

"She lucky I don't beat her ass," Tyne said, watching Neeci walk by the front of her car.

"What the fuck you say?" Neeci snapped back. She turned around and came closer. Her high-pitched voice was truly one of a kind. "Girl, I know you wasn't talkin' to me?"

Dressed in a short skirt – on a fall day in Indianapolis – and a shirt that did little to hide her chest, Neeci walked up as if she was the baddest chick in the entire Midwest.

"And if I was talkin' to you?" Tyne asked as she slammed her car door and walked up onto the sidewalk. "Girl, you know I ain't been cool with yo ugly, big-lip ass since I caught you out here try'na drop to your knees and suck on my nigga's dick. You may have sucked all these other chick's dicks around here, but you really need to stay away from mine."

"Girl, I know your kind," Neeci said, looking Tyne up and down. "You cute… a little. But you ain't got shit on me." She leaned in closer. "And that's why you actin' the way you actin'. You already know that if I get my hands on, or should I say my lips on, that fine all yellow nigga you got comin' over here, he gon' forget who the fuck he even used to know over here." Neeci pointed her finger in Tyne's face. "Facts."

Ronnisha stood quietly, but she knew that something was about to pop off. One thing she had learned about her best friend early on was that she was not the kind of person to just let some chick put her finger in her face.

Within the blink of an eye, Tyne had reached out and slapped Neeci across the face. The slap was so loud that the entire parking lot could hear it, especially at this early hour of the day when traffic in the area was low and the children had already gotten on their school buses.

"Bitch, watch how the fuck you talk to me!" Tyne yelled. She dropped her McDonald's bag and put her hands up. "I been waitin' to beat your ass. You one of them bitches that deserves this shit you got comin'. I heard about you. All you do is suck dick."

Grabbing the side of her face, Neeci leaned back up. Immediately, she began swinging at Tyne. However, she wasn't fast enough. Before she knew it, Tyne had grabbed a handful of her weave and pulled her head down to the hood of the car.

"Stop you crazy, bitch!" Neeci said, feeling powerless to stop it. "Stop! Stop! Stop her!" She looked at Ronnisha, who was standing back and watching. When it came to fighting, Tyne never needed any help.

Ronnisha watched as Tyne pulled clumps of Neeci's weave out of her head. She kept her grip tight and kept Neeci's head pressed against the hood of the car. She slapped her back and forth, on both sides of the face, as Neeci's arms flailed about.

"Now what, bitch?" Tyne asked. "Now what? I'mma fuck this face up so bad that you not gon' even be able to open your mouth wide enough to suck one of these nigga's dicks. You ain't goin' nowhere."

39

"No, please," Neeci pleaded. It was too late, however. Tyne continued on with the whooping, only letting up when her hand began to hurt. Neeci quickly moved out of Tyne's path. "Fuck you, you bitch! You just crazy." She grabbed the sides of her face, feeling tears streaming down her cheeks.

Tyne jumped forward, causing Neeci to jump back. Neeci then turned around and walked away, feeling humiliated. Further down the parking lot, at entrances to other buildings, guys stepped out in just their basketball shorts and flip flips and watched. Neeci soon enough disappeared.

Ronnisha looked at Tyne. "Damn, girl, you ain't have to do all that to the girl," she said.

"Shit, girl, whatever," Tyne said. "She came to me and startin' talkin' stupid, and she try'na get at the one nigga that I'm actually kinda feeling in a long time. She lucky I went easy on her and we got to go to my family later on or else I woulda really wore her ass out… I woulda sent that ass home really cryin' and beat up, don't play with me like that. She just learned her lesson and she learned it the hard way."

Ronnisha giggled, following Tyne into the apartment. She shook her head once they had stepped inside and were eating their McDonald's. "Damn, that dick got you gone I can see, girl," she said. "Hmm, hmm."

Tyne snickered as she bit into her breakfast sandwich. She then shrugged and said, "It's so big and juicy too, girl. Damn."

Once they'd finished eating breakfast, they chilled for a lot of the day, which Ronnisha hadn't had a chance to do with Tyne in a long time. Tyne worked quite a bit at the hotel, so it was rare for her to actually wind up with a day off during the week. Ronnisha, waiting to hear back from Danez, went with Tyne to run some errands. This took up most of the afternoon. They then stopped by the mall, but Ronnisha didn't buy anything. She knew that it would only be a matter of time, especially after having to flee her own apartment like some refugee in the middle of the night, that Danez would be taking her shopping once again. And she knew very well that he would buy her whatever she pointed at, and then some.

"Girl, you sure you wanna go with me to this get together?" Tyne asked Ronnisha as 6pm was approaching. "I mean, you know how my family can be. They all dry and stuff."

"What is the get together for again?" Ronnisha asked.

Tyne shrugged. "Shit, I don't know," she answered. "Probably somebody had a bunch of food that's about to go bad or something like that, so they just figured we could have a family function and somebody eat it all."

"Yeah, girl," Ronnisha said. "I'll go, like I told you this morning. Plus, I like your family."

Tyne looked at Ronnisha with a disgusted face. "Girl, they okay," she said. "I mean, they don't really talk about much and they kinda self-centered and stuff, but I guess from the outside looking in you might look at them and see a bunch of calm people."

"Exactly, girl," Ronnisha said, taking a moment to think of her own family. "Calm is what I like. Them niggas I got in my family…" She shook her head as her words trailed off. "Good God Almighty, them niggas keep so much shit goin' sometime that even bein' in the same city as them makes me get a headache. I do gotta go over there later on for my little niece's birthday party. She mean everything to me, or else I wouldn't be goin'. They not startin' it till eight because they gotta wait for my sister to get off work."

Ronnisha decided that she'd follow Tyne to her mother's house so that she could leave and be on time for her niece's birthday party. As usually, once Ronnisha arrived, she was greeted in a very warm way by all of Tyne's relatives. Halfway through the family function, around 7 o'clock, as they sat around the dining room table in the Victorian home not too far to the east of downtown, Ronnisha felt her phone vibrating in her pocket. As to not draw too much attention to herself, she slid it out and saw that Danez was calling. She looked up at Tyne's family and said, "Excuse me. I gotta take this phone call."

"No problem, Ronnisha," Tyne's Aunt Beverly said. "Just go on and step into the front room or somethin'. Won't nobody bother you."

Ronnisha thanked Beverly then quickly stepped into the living room. Tyne's family had always called this room "The White Room." The furniture was clearly much older, if not antique. Without a doubt, it was worth far more money than whatever everybody else would buy at Value City. Small figurines were places about on the coffee table and end tables.

"Hello?" Ronnisha answered.

"Wassup, Baby?" Danez said. "How you?"

"I'm good, I guess," Ronnisha said, watching her voice as to not speak too loudly. "How did everything go?"

"Well," Danez said. "I called Lamarcus's mama, so she up here now. You shoulda seen her face when she got here and saw Lamarcus."

"Damn," Ronnisha said, "is he that fucked up like that?"

Danez hesitated. "It's pretty bad," he said. "I ain't even wanna leave the hospital 'cause, well, that shit coulda been me instead of him."

"Yeah, but you can't think that way," Ronnisha said. "I mean, it wasn't you and just be happy that it wasn't. So, you been up at the hospital all this time?"

"Yes and no," Danez said. "The doctors said that he gon' be okay, but he ingested or whatever a lot of his own blood, so that was going to cause some kinda problem. Shit, I don't know what the fuck they was talkin' about. I went home for a minute this morning to just check on the house and stuff... You know, see if anybody was in there or something like that, after you left."

"And?" Ronnisha asked, fearing a small rivet of fear run through her body. "It ain't look like nobody came up in there after I left, did it?"

"Naw," Danez said, in a very matter of fact way. "You ain't gotta worry about that, so just calm down. Plus, them niggas would have to be bold as fuck to just walk up in that building knowing that not only is it in the heart of downtown, but it also has security and a doorman and people like that working in there. You seen Lamarcus's grandma's house where he live now, over on the east side, right?"

"Yeah," Ronnisha said, nodding as she remembered a small party that Lamarcus had over there during the holiday season. "It's in the city, but isolated, I guess you could say."

"Exactly," Danez said. "But, like I was sayin'.... I went home for a little bit and just ain't feel right leavin' Lamarcus' mother up here. His face is so busted up. I mean, the nigga basically look like he about to be dead. But, you already know what I'm thinkin'." Danez's voice lowered as it sounded as if he were walking further away from something. "I'm thinkin' this chick he had there had something to do with it, but I ain't wanna say nothin'."

"What chick?" Ronnisha asked. "Danez, you ain't tell me that Lamarcus had some chick over there when you found him."

"Ronnisha, you know that nigga always keep some chick around him," Danez said. "Shit, it's like that nigga goes to Walmart and picks one out off of a shelf whenever his dick get hard. But this chick, her name is Rain... This is the chick he was tellin' me that he actually catchin' feelins for."

"I see," Ronnisha said, a bit impressed. Lamarcus had never come across as the kind of guy who would ever consider settling down, let alone doing so at a young age when he and his boy were out in the streets and making real money for the first time in their lives. "But, Danez, what make you think that she did it? And what the fuck was she doin' when you got there and stuff? Was she even still there?"

"Yeah, the chick was still there," Danez said. "But, naw, on the way to the hospital, I took her too. But she was only knocked out, I guess, on the couch. All she said that she remember is seein' them shoot the house up and shit and next thing she knew she was knocked out and woke up on the couch in the front room where you enter the house. I just got a bad feeling about her because of when I was talkin' to her on our way over to the hospital and shit."

"Oh, yeah?" Ronnisha said, wondering what this Rain chick could have said to make Danez suspicious. Danez had always been rather good at picking up on different things, which was something that Ronnisha liked about him. "What she say?"

"I was talkin' about how I wanna know how the fuck Qoree and his niggas would have even found out where Lamarcus live," Danez explained. "Right then, I noticed how she got real quiet, especially for somebody that supposedly was just as much a victim as this nigga. Somethin' up about her, Ronnisha. And I just don't know what, but somethin' tellin' me that she mighta had something to do with this. Plus, when I was talkin' to her and shit, she looked out the window like she was thinkin' about something else. I don't know, maybe I'm trippin'."

"I don't know," Ronnisha said. "I mean, I met the chick that one time, but I ain't really get to talk to her or nothin' like that to get a vibe from her. Why you even think that she would have a part in some shit like this, Danez? I mean, I guess it is possible and stuff. I ain't gon' say that it's not. But, at the same time, if the house and

43

shit got shot up while she was there and shit too, why would she set it up to happen when she was there when she just coulda had that shit done after she left or somethin'?"

"Yeah, I feel you on that," Danez said. "I don't know. I still gotta do some thinkin'. I miss you, Baby. And I'm ready to come home and see you. I miss you."

Ronnisha smiled, feeling her heart warm up. "I miss you too," she said. "Right now, I'm at Tyne's family house. They had a little thing today and since I hadn't heard from you yet, and I ain't know if goin' back home would be okay and shit, I decided to come over here with her. I wasn't doin' nothin' else and she happened to be off today, so I was like why not. Then, in a little bit, I'mma roll up on out of here and go over to my auntie house for Nalia's birthday party."

"Fuck, I forgot about that," Danez said. "I thought that shit was tomorrow night or somethin' like that."

"I forgot too until earlier," Ronnisha said.

"Did you still want me to come with you?" Danez asked.

Ronnisha took a moment to think about it. She had to take into consideration how her family viewed Danez, as well as what they thought about her dating him. "I mean," she said. "You can if you want to, but you really ain't got to. You know how them niggas is. I'm just gon' be over there for a little bit. Then, I'mma be home."

"Bet," Danez said. "I'mma be back at the apartment in a little bit too. I was try'na wait on my boy to wake up and shit so I could talk to him, but the doctors came out earlier and told us some shit about how that might not be until tomorrow."

"Okay," Ronnisha said. "Then we can go up there together or something, maybe?"

"Yep," Danez said. "Oh, shit, here come the doctor. I'll text you in a little bit, okay?"

"Okay," Ronnisha said. She hung up the phone and went back into the dining room to continue socializing with Tyne's lovely family – a family she wished her own would be more similar to. While she sat there enjoying this meal, she had no way of knowing that things were going on beyond her reach – things that would soon reach out and affect her in ways she would have never thought to be possible.

44

CHAPTER 5

When Danez hung up the phone, he turned around to find that the doctor was speaking with Lamarcus' mother, Amber. The look on the doctor's face said it all. Without thinking, and because Lamarcus was practically like a brother to him, Danez rushed over to Amber and stood at her side. Once the doctor checked with Amber to make sure that it was okay for Danez to stand there and listen to whatever was about to be said, she continued.

"Miss Rogers," Doctor Adair said, "this is not going as well as we would have hoped."

Amber's heart sunk; Danez's rage increased. Amber lifted her hand up and placed it over her mouth. "What?" she asked. "What do you mean it didn't go as well as you thought it would or hoped it would? What are you talkin' about? My baby ain't gon' die, is he?"

Doctor Adair took a deep breath. She glanced away for a moment then back to Amber. "Well, Miss Rogers, we are doing all we can," she said. "Please, try not to worry too much. However, I must say that this is one of the worst beatings we've seen in quite some time here. A lot of damage was done to Lamarcus's body, not only externally but also internally."

"Okay," Amber said, trying to make some sense of what she was being told. "So, what are you saying? What's the deal, Doctor? Look, I appreciate you trying to be cordial about this with me and stuff, but I really just want to know."

"Okay," the doctor said. "Well, as you already know, your son lost a lot of blood. We are also finding that there is nerve damage."

"Nerve damage?" Amber said. "Okay, so what does that mean?"

"Basically, Miss Rogers," the doctor began, "nerves are what tell your body parts to do this and do that. For example," she pointed at the ground, "do you see how we are standing here right now?"

"Yes," Amber said, nodding her head. "Okay, okay."

"Okay, well, because of nerves," the doctor went on, "we are able to tell our legs to stand up. Without them, we'd fall down to the ground every time we tried to stand up because the message would not be getting to the feet and legs. It works the same way with balling your fists. Your brain is sending a message to your hands and telling them to ball up rather than lay flat. Well, that is where the problem is for your son. The beating was so bad that some of his nerves were damaged in his legs, back, and arms. From what we can see, some of the nerves will recover on their own. Other nerves, however, will need to be operated on."

"Operated on?" Amber said, sounding very worried. "Doctor, I don't know if we got that kinda money. I don't even think my son had health insurance that would cover something like that. I mean, what do we do?"

"That's not what I wanted you to hear, Miss Rogers," Doctor Adair said. "What I need for you, and Lamarcus, once he wakes up, to understand, is that the surgeries we are talking about, to get to the nerves we are talking about, have a fifty-fifty chance of being successful. In really depends on the person's health and genetics, if you want the honest truth."

"Hold up, Doctor," Danez interjected. "So, what do that mean?"

The doctor looked into Danez eyes for a couple of seconds too long, letting him know that she was about to come with an answer he wouldn't like.

"It means that whatever those nerves control," Doctor Adair said, "will suffer greatly. One I can tell you about right now is his speech. The nerve that controlled that, Miss Rogers, was severely damaged."

Amber practically fell into Danez's shoulder upon hearing that. "Are you serious?" she asked. "So, that mean that if the surgery don't work, he won't be able to talk right?"

Rather than answer with words, the doctor nodded.

Amber looked at Danez then back to the doctor. She told the doctor to do whatever she could to fix her son. As they watched the doctor walk away, Amber, who looked as exhausted as she felt, turned to Danez. His nostrils flared, letting her know that he was severely upset.

"Danez," Amber said. "Danez, Baby. Don't go doin' nothin' stupid."

"Oh, it ain't gon' be stupid, Miss Amber," Danez said, shaking his head. "It's not gon' be stupid at all."

Danez had started to walk away but was quickly pulled back by Amber. "Danez, what is going on?" she asked. "I feel like something is goin' on that you not tellin' me."

"I was almost gon' go back to the house last night, Miss Amber," Danez said, "but I changed my mind."

"Back to my mama's house?" Amber asked. "Why, Danez?"

"Cause," Danez said, "I had a funny suspicion. Well, a couple. Rain, the chick your son is talkin' to, already told me who did this stuff. It was this nigga name Qoree."

"Qoree?" Amber asked. "Who in the world is Qoree? I ain't never heard of nobody named Qoree. And why would he come for my son like this and go this hard?"

Since Danez didn't know how much Lamarcus' mother knew about his life, he still wanted to shield her from knowing anything that could taint her son's image to her. Amber picked up on Danez' hesitation. In light of such, she said, "Keep it real with me, Danez. I know what my son be doin'. I know. I know the shit ain't right, but I know what he be doin'."

"Well," Danez said. "When we started moving more and more, um, work in The Land, supposedly we got in on this dude Qoree's territory. All them niggas over there, off of Clifton and MLK, say they hate the nigga and that he was basically bein' ran outta the streets over there. Long story short, I guess that ain't the case. Somehow, he found out where Lamarcus stay and decided to come and do this shit – stuff, I mean. Excuse me. The money was gone when I went back by the house last night. The money was gone."

"The money was gone?" Amber asked. "What money? He had money stashed over at the house?"

"You know the spare room in the basement where there's like a bookshelf and a bed, I think?" Danez asked. "Well, he got a safe behind there where he kept all his money. I was gon' go check and see if the money was gone, but I know the police would prolly be there. And you know I don't like dealin' with them if I can help it."

"This was a set up?" Amber said, shaking her head. She then turned and looked back at Lamarcus' room, down the hall. "I always told him to watch who he hang out with and to not have nobody over to his place unless he got to. I feel like this is my fault. I was lettin' him help me pay for my house and pay off some of my debt and shit, not thinkin' about how deep he was getting into this mess." Her eyes swelled with tears. "I can't believe I helped him get to this point."

"Don't blame yourself, Miss Amber," Danez said. "I mean, we gon' get that nigga Qoree."

"Danez, don't go getting yourself killed," Amber pleaded. "You know how much I like your mama and stuff, and I definitely don't want her to have to go through what I'm goin' through right now by seein' her son in some hospital, or worse."

"Naw," Danez said. "That ain't gon' happen. Trust me, Miss Amber, it's better we do this than the police. 'Cause you know how the police are out here nowadays. They be findin' ways to lock everybody up for somethin' that one nigga did. I told them as little as I could last night, and that was only because the doctor went ahead and called them and stuff. You know I ain't do no stuff like that. So," he leaned in and talked to Miss Amber in a very domineering way, to let her know how serious the situation was, "don't go sayin' nothin' to the police." He looked up and around to make sure that nobody was eavesdropping on their conversation. "And don't you worry, we gon' make sure this is all clean so you ain't got to worry about that nigga Qoree again, okay?"

On that note, Danez walked away. He had talked to he and Lamarcus' boys Marquis and Nieko, both of whom were going to come up to the hospital once they'd gotten off work. Danez remembered that they were supposedly getting off work at 7 o'clock, which had just passed. He pulled his phone out of his pocket and called Nieko. "Nigga, where the fuck y'all at?" he asked Nieko when he answered.

"Shit, I'm 'bout to swoop up Marquis and we gon' be on our way up there and shit like we told you earlier, my nigga," Nieko said. His strong Harlem accent came through the phone, which was at times a little difficult for Danez to understand.

"Bet," Danez said. "I was just checkin' to make sure. I'll meet y'all niggas out in the parking lot and shit so we can talk about this shit."

Nieko agreed and hung up. Danez went down to the first floor and hurried out into the parking lot. There, he messaged what he'd just found out to Ronnisha. Several minutes later, Nieko's black Sentra, which belonged to his mother, turned into the hospital parking lot. Danez watched him park on the outer edge of the lot then the two of them – Nieko and Marquis – walked quickly up to the hospital entrance. Nieko, who was darker-skinned and somewhat round with dyed brown dreads, hugged and shook hands with Danez. Then, Marquis, who was tall and thin with a long nose, crayon-brown skin, and gold snatch-outs, did the same.

"What the fuck, my nigga?" Nieko asked. "Is he gon' be okay? Can we go in and see him?"

"The doctor will let you see him, but it ain't a pretty sight," Danez said. "Lamarcus is pretty fucked up. The doctor herself even said that it had been a while since she seen some shit this bad."

Danez spent the next several minutes going over the entire story again. This time, he was much more relaxed and passionate as Nieko and Marquis were probably the only two dudes in the entire city that he and Lamarcus felt like they could trust. Danez went over not only what the doctor said, which caused all three of their hearts to hurt from just thinking about it, but also about how he'd found the money missing. The very thought of how much money Qoree could have gotten away with was enough to make Nieko and Marquis angry. Then, Danez went on to explain his suspicious feelings about the Rain chick. The three of them talked about how if she were truly a victim with him, and the two had been getting kind of serious, there was no reason that she shouldn't be up at the hospital as well. In fact, some could even argue, as Marquis explained, that Lamarcus took the beating so that she would be okay. Danez found it odd that she got help late last night, came upstairs for a few minutes to cry alongside Miss Amber, then left as if she had somewhere to be.

When Danez had finished filling Marquis and Nieko in on what was going on, he knew he needed to go make some money as well as check on his business over on the west side. Even though the guilt was there, as he was leaving his boy in the hospital all beaten up, he knew the businesses had to keep going and he had to keep making his money. Before he walked off to get into his car and allow Marquis and Nieko to go up and see Lamarcus, he stopped them and said, "Watch y'all back, niggas. When I hit y'all up later on tonight, I want y'all to answer. I'm tellin' you, that Rain chick give me a bad feelin' and I really feel like she had somethin' to do with this shit."

"We feel you," Nieko said.

"And I'mma fuckin' find out how Qoree found out where Lamarcus stay," Danez said, "and where the fuck he took the money. We gon' get that money back. Fuck that nigga. We gettin' Lamarcus' money back if nothin' else. And stay packin' some heat.

We don't know who the fuck been talkin' too much, and what names they said." He watched Nieko and Marquis nod their heads. "I'mma be up with Ronnisha later on and shit, so just hit me up and we can talk and shit and figure out what we gotta do. And makes sure y'all niggas let me know if that Rain chick come back up here, okay?"

CHAPTER 6

In many ways, it was hard for Ronnisha to leave Tyne's family function. She always had such a nice time with Tyne's family, and this time was no exception to that. When Ronnisha climbed into her car, happy that she'd driven herself, she knew she needed to stop somewhere between where she was and where her Aunt Kim lived to buy some sort of gift for her niece, Nalia. She looked through her purse and found eleven one hundred-dollar bills that Danez had given to her just a few days before. She smiled thinking about Danez and how much he loved and supported her. Ronnisha liked even more that he was there for Lamarcus in his time of need, as it showed good character. In fact, Ronnisha had already made up her mind to do whatever it took to help Danez, however she could, because Lamarcus just didn't deserve somebody to do something like that to him. Lamarcus was a really good dude, who never made a pass at her or anything like that.

Ronnisha wound up stopping at a Toys-R-Us to buy Nalia a mermaid doll, remembering how fascinated the little girl was with the idea that mermaids actually existed. When Ronnisha babysat for her sister, she would often listen to Nalia talked about different articles on mermaids she'd read online. While Ronnisha certainly didn't believe in mermaids, or didn't care enough to form any sort of opinion, she simply wanted to encourage her niece to think. After she purchased the mermaid doll, she headed over to her Aunt Kim's house. Ronnisha could feel the anxiety building in her, as she hoped this late-in-the-evening birthday party would be peaceful and drama free. These feelings were so strong that Ronnisha's head shook as she turned into the suburban-like subdivision where her Aunt Kim now lived.

Because Ronnisha's mother had run out to be with some man when Ronnisha was a young girl, she was raised by her Aunt Kim. Her father would pop up every once in a while, but he was by no means a beacon of any sort of stability – not by the furthest stretch of the imagination. Over the last couple of years, Ronnisha's relationship with her Aunt Kim had been somewhat rocky. Part of the reason was because Ronnisha decided to not go to college, which was something that Kim had drilled into her niece's head. Perhaps she pushed the idea so much that it made Ronnisha want to push away from it. When Ronnisha started talking to then dating Danez,

Kim's mouth began to get looser and looser. This looseness only got worse when Kim finally met Danez and had a talk with him, finding so many holes in his sources of income that she would often say, "Stevie Wonder could see that nigga is up to some shit that he ain't got no business being up to." Later on down the road, when Kim found out that Ronnisha was moving in with this Danez guy, rather than continuing her education or even, at least, getting a job, there was a full-blown falling out between the two. Since then, communication was somewhat regular, but also strained.

As Ronnisha pulled into a parking spot out in front of Kim's four-bedroom, cookie-cutter house, she looked up at the house. "Please," she said out loud, looking at the driveway full of cars. "I hope these niggas don't start no shit with me today. They already lucky that I'm even comin' around they asses."

Ronnisha then relaxed, thinking that maybe she was overthinking it all. Instead, she put on her best self and headed into the house. Immediately, upon walking in, she was greeted by her cousins, her niece Nalia, and her half-sister, Brineesha. Ronnisha, deciding to be the bigger person and not act toward her sister the way she had been acting toward her, smiled and hugged her. "Girl, you look good," Ronnisha said, patting Brineesha on the back. "Real good."

"You too, Ronnisha," Brineesha said. She then stopped, stood back for a moment, and looked at Ronnisha. "I see you still ain't had that man's baby yet. I thought you would by now, girl. You really are surprising me."

Ronnisha squinted at her half-sister Brineesha, who was several years older. The two had grown up knowing one another rather well, despite not growing up in the same house. Because Brineesha had a different father, her life wound up being drastically different from Ronnisha's life. When their mother had run off with her boyfriend, Brineesha was able to go live with her father. Soon after, her father went back to school to get his degree and was able to come into a pretty good paying job. Down the road, this helped Brineesha because her father had groomed her to strive for a career in something. Brineesha wound up going to Indiana University, having only graduated a couple of years ago. Soon after college, she met her husband, George, who worked in banking.

Ronnisha, not going to let her sister get to her, turned away and ignored her. She went to the kitchen, where the family was congregated, and said hello to everyone. Once she'd finished with the hugs, she sat down at the dining room table and sung Happy Birthday with the family. Not soon after the song ended and the family had begun to cut into the cake, Nalia looked at her Auntie Ronnisha and asked, "Auntie Ronny, when are you going to have some kids?"

Ronnisha chuckled nervously and blushed. Just as she was opening her mouth to answer, Brineesha had cut her off. "That's just what I was saying, Nalia," she said. "I thought she would have had one by now. She's already living with the man. I was so sure that they'd be starting a family and whatnot together."

With Nalia's eyes watching her, Ronnisha couldn't help but to bite her lip. She cracked a smile and looked at her niece. "I'm not ready yet," she responded. "I'm waiting until I grow the fuck up. I see some people around here still ain't done that."

"I know she ain't talkin' about me," Brineesha said, shaking her head. Just then, the woman stood up. "I know she is not talking to me and she is the one over there dating the thug and not working, again."

Ignoring the advice of the older family members around the table to calm down, Ronnisha stood up and pointed at Brineesha. "Girl, just cause you married some nigga that work at a fuckin' bank, don't make you no betta than me," she said. "I don't know where you get off actin' like that, but girl with how that face look, you should be lucky that you even found a man that wanted to get in the bed with you. You damn near won the lottery finding one that wanted to marry you. I know you livin' up in that white neighborhood and stuff, but I just hope that," she glanced down and Nalia, knowing that she should be careful with how she ended this sentence, "he doesn't get acquainted with Becky down the street." Ronnisha smiled.

Brineesha, shaking her head, began to make her way around the table. Immediately, Kim, who was always tall for her height and big boned, stood up. She planted her hands into Brineesha's shoulders and pushed her back. "Girl, think about it," she said. "You got too much to lose by fightin' her. Too much to lose."

All Ronnisha could do was shake her head. She'd always seen the difference in how she was treated by Aunt Kim compared to her half-sister. In fact, Ronnisha always thought of the treatment as being completely opposite. While Ronnisha was like the black sheep of the family because she fell in love with a thug who had a good heart, Brineesha was like the chosen one—the star of the family. Rarely did anyone say anything negative about her, especially once she began moving up in life.

Aunt Kim turned to Ronnisha with a scorned look. "Ronnisha," she said, pointing at the kitchen. "Let me talk to you real quick."

Ronnisha, standing firm in her place, looked around. The eyes around the table were watching her. She then decided that it was for the best if she just went along with things and talked to her Aunt Kim in the kitchen. As she turned around and headed into the kitchen, she shook her head and mumbled under her breath, "I swear if this bitch say the wrong thing to me."

Kim quickly came into the kitchen as the family continued on with the birthday party, trying to help Nalia forget about what she'd just seen happen between her mother and aunt. Kim looked back at the family then to Ronnisha. "Ronnisha," she said, "girl, what is wrong with you?"

"What you mean what is wrong with me?" Ronnisha asked. "Who said that there was anything wrong with me? I don't even know why you try'na talk to me like I'm the one who started that shit in there or somethin'. You saw it, didn't you? I only been here for like an hour and that's the second little snobby comment she done made to me already."

"Ronnisha," Kim said, "I understand. But you can't go goin' off like that and causin' a scene over something as small as that. Think about it, Ronnisha. Will you? You coulda ruined that little girl's birthday party."

"I coulda ruined it?" Ronnisha asked. "Are you serious? You really try'na blame this on me. In fact, what you need to be doin' is bringin' the princess of the family in here and havin' a talk with her."

Kim paused and shook her head. She looked Ronnisha up and down, noticing how the ripped blue jeans she wore were so tight around her thighs. At the rips, the fat of her thighs was bulging out.

She then looked up at Ronnisha's chest and how too much of it was showing, especially for a birthday party. It was very clear to Kim that she was losing her niece that she had raised all on her own to the street life. She began to shake her head, only thinking about how she wanted better for Ronnisha, if nothing else.

"What is going on with you, Ronnisha?" Kim asked. "When are you going to do something with your life?"

"What you mean when am I gonna do something with my life?" Ronnisha asked, feeling insulted. "Y'all act like I stand on a corner downtown or at some highway exit shaking a cup for some coins and am happy when I get some dollar bills. What you mean, Aunt Kim?"

"I mean, when are you going to move on from that nigga you call yourself dating and actually do something with your life?" Kim asked.

Ronnisha pressed the palm of her left hand into the kitchen counter and looked away. With her eyes practically rolled to the back of her head, she looked back at Kim. "That nigga I call myself dating?" she asked, shaking her head. "Aunt Kim, that nigga's name is Danez. You met him and stuff."

"I don't give a fuck what that nigga's name is," Kim said, shaking her head. She then reached up and repositioned her wig ever so slightly. "I know when I met him, I could see that he was no good. I know he, supposedly, own them little stores and stuff over on the west side. I been by them, don't think that I haven't. And that nigga ain't makin' that kinda money for the two of you to be livin' the good life, up next to them white people downtown. I ain't stupid, Ronnisha. I know how much that stuff downtown is renting for. And some of the math just ain't adding up for me."

"I told you, Aunt Kim," Ronnisha said, just wanting her aunt to stop bringing up what she had with Danez. "He ain't doin' nothin' funny, okay? He is just good with his money and stuff. That's all. He don't sell no drugs or nothin' like that."

Kim stepped away, shaking her head. Halfway across the room, she turned around. "You must really think I'm stupid, don't you?" she asked. "Give it up, Ronnisha. I can see right through you. It's a shame, girl. It's really sad. You live off that nigga and you know he not makin' his money right. Girl, what do you think is gon' eventually happen with you? You know you gon' get caught up in

56

some shit because of that little nigga. Then what? You're going to be looking stupid like all of these other chicks you see on the news and stuff, going down because they were helping their boyfriend or something like that?"

"This ain't that, Aunt Kim," Ronnisha said, wanting her aunt to stay out of her business. Danez was too smart to ever get caught up in his game, and she was too clever to be a victim should such a thing ever happen and her own life be at stake. "Me and Danez love each other. He would never do anything that could get me hurt, so I don't even know why you're thinking that."

"'Cause, Ronnisha," Kim said. "You ain't got no job, but you always in a nice car, got new hair, nice clothes, and jewelry. Money don't grow on trees. And if it did, you ain't even got a yard to plant the tree in. How are you all paying for all of this?"

Ronnisha looked dead into her Aunt Kim's eyes, unmoving. "Don't worry about all that," she said. "Let Ronnisha and Danez worry about Ronnisha and Danez, okay? You just mad 'cause you never found a man to help take care of you."

Before Kim could respond, Ronnisha walked out of the kitchen and back into the dining area. After the family looked at her for a moment, seeing the emotion in her face, everyone went on talking as they had been moments before. For the next thirty minutes or so, Ronnisha joined in the conversation and carried on as if not a damn thing in the world was bothering her. She wasn't going to let her Aunt Kim ruin her spirits because she chose to side with Brineesha. Even more so, Brineesha wasn't going to keep looking down on her when the fact of the matter was that Ronnisha had the better life, and the better looks and body.

Around 8:30, there was a knock at the front door. Immediately, Ronnisha looked up, wondering who it could be. Most of her family sat around the table already. And the people who were not there weren't the types to be coming at nearly 9 o'clock at night. Kim jumped up and rushed to the front door to open it. Once it opened, Ronnisha felt her heart stop. She had to look away, as the person who came walking in was her father.

"What the hell is that nigga doin' here?" Ronnisha asked herself, practically whispering.

Ronnisha's father, Greg, walked into the house and quickly slid out of his jacket. Kim walked him into the dining area, where the entire family sat, and reminded everyone of who he was, in case their memory needed a little refresher. The 50-year-old man with a gray beard and round glasses, standing at just under 6 feet tall, came around to Ronnisha's side of the table and stood there. Ronnisha could feel the eyes of her family members. They barreled down on her as she didn't want to move, but wanted to know at the same time why her father was even present in the first place. He'd never been much of a family person, which was obvious from how Ronnisha had grown up, that it was quite odd for him to be at the birthday party of someone who was not even a relative of his.

Hesitantly, Ronnisha stood up to hug her father. "Hey, Daddy," she said. "How you doin'?"

"Hey, Baby Girl," Greg said, chuckling. "I ain't think you was gon' stand up and speak to your daddy. Nice to see you, Ronnisha."

"Nice to see you too, Daddy," Ronnisha said, sitting back down.

The party went on for the next hour or so. Ronnisha watched as different people left, citing the reason being that they had to be at work the next morning. Eventually, Brineesha, still riding on her high horse, left with Nalia. She thanked Kim for having the party at her house since it was closer to the city and easier for everybody to get to. Around 10 o'clock, Ronnisha was about ready to go herself. She began to slide into her jacket when her father came walking into the living room.

"You not gon' just leave without sayin' bye, are you?" Greg asked.

Ronnisha looked at her father and rolled her eyes. "Well," she said, "I learned from the best on how to do that, so I thought you would know what was going down. That's all."

Greg pressed his lips together. He knew he wasn't exactly the best father to Ronnisha, and he accepted full responsibility for that. However, he didn't come to make amends with her, as that would take time – months and months, if not years. Rather, he came to talk to her about what Kim had been telling him. Greg glanced back at Kim before looking back at Ronnisha. "Ronnisha," he said, "what's goin' on with you, Baby Girl? I hear you just kinda livin' up with some nigga and stuff?"

"Huh?" Ronnisha asked, not believing her father's audacity. "What do you even know about my life enough to come here, after I ain't even seen your black ass for like a year, and be askin' me what is goin' on with my relationship? Huh, Daddy? Shit, I shouldn't even be callin' you that if you wanna know the truth. I should be callin' you the guy that got my mother pregnant."

Hearing such a comment did indeed sting, but he pushed on so he could find out if what he'd heard about his daughter was true. "Okay, fair enough," he said, "but I hear that the dude you livin' with and playin' wifey with might be one of these niggas out in the streets, Ronnisha."

"Who told you that?" Ronnisha asked. "Huh? You been talkin' to Aunt Kim, ain't you?"

Greg glanced at her. "I keep up on you, Ronnisha," he said. "I know you don't think I care and stuff, but I do."

"Then, if you care, Daddy," Ronnisha said, "then why wasn't you there for me? Why wasn't you there? You can't just pop up in my life and act like I'm supposed to give you updates on what's goin' on, just because Aunt Kim ole desperate ass say that there is somethin' goin' on. And, like I told her, y'all ain't got to worry about Danez."

"So, you just his ride or die chick, huh?" Greg asked. "You might as well go on and tell me at least that, Baby Girl. Is that what you got goin' on? I heard you not workin' right now and ain't even tryin' to. Is that what you supposed to be? You supposed to be his ride or die chick and stuff? You know that shit ain't gon' end good for you. It never do."

"Shit," Ronnisha said, feeling brazen and brave. "It look like it gon' end betta for me than knowin' you did. Look what happened with you, why don't you? You was supposed to be my daddy. Mama runs off to be with some other niggas, and I ain't seen her in years, so what happens? Instead of goin' to my daddy, like a child should go to if they mother ain't around, I wound up goin' to my auntie. And now you wanna show up and play daddy like I'm supposed to care." Ronnisha picked up her purse then pulled the front door open. Autumn wind rushed into the house, blowing her hair back. "Fuck off, nigga," she added.

"Ronnisha, listen to me when I at least say this," Greg said. "Based on what I'm hearin', that nigga is not gon' turn out good for you. It's only gon' be a matter of time before it all caves in on you, Ronnisha. It's only gon' be—"

Ronnisha had slammed the door before her father could finish what he was saying. Feeling angry that she'd come to the birthday party, and even angrier than she'd stayed long enough to essentially be embarrassed twice, she rushed down to her car. Once inside, she quickly turned the engine over and let out a deep sigh. She leaned back into her headrest then looked up at her Aunt Kim's house. She felt deep down inside that Danez was really all she had in this world. Her own family didn't believe in her, and would say anything to put her down. Shaking her head, she pulled off and headed toward the nearest busy road. On her way home, she pulled her phone out and called Danez. He was the only person in the world who understood her and she needed to talk to him right away.

CHAPTER 7

Feeling sprinkles of rain come down and get into her hair, Rain rushed into Community Hospital East. Just that morning, she'd been treated for her injuries, which were very mild, and released. After going upstairs to check on Lamarcus, as well as say hi to his mother Amber, she'd gone home with so much on her mind. Exhausted, and in some pain from the blow she'd taken to the head that had knocked her unconscious, Rain had gone home to get some sleep. The very first thing she'd thought about when she'd woken up in the afternoon was Lamarcus. She hoped that he was okay as she went about her day, getting things done. Once she'd gone to help her mother with something, she made her way up to the hospital. She hoped that a lot of people would not be outside of his room. If this were the case, she'd be ten times as nervous as she already was.

Rain made her way up the elevator. As soon as she stepped off of the elevator, she looked at Amber and two of Lamarcus' friends sitting in the waiting area. Amber watched as Rain, who was dressed in a cute beige trench coat and some high boots that looked very European, hurried over.

"Hi," Rain said, smiling. "I got back up here as soon as I could."

Amber, Marquis, and Nieko looked at Rain. Each of them, while being tightlipped and cold, thought about what Danez said. While they didn't know if Danez's theory that Rain had set all of this up was completely true, they knew Danez well enough to respect what he thought and at least act as if it were true.

"Oh, you okay, Rain," Amber said. She too had begun to pick up on something about Rain. She seemed like a sweet girl, but she was a little too clingy to be a chick that hadn't really been properly introduced to her "man's" mother. "I'm just sittin' up here myself. I'mma probably go home in a little bit myself since there's nothing I can do here."

"Has he woken up?" Rain asked, looking back at the entrance that led to a hallway of hospital rooms.

Amber shook her head. "Naw," she answered. "He ain't woke up yet. The doctors said they had to operate on him, and I hope that they work out, for Lamarcus's sake." Amber knew she wanted to see how Rain reacted to certain key phrases. "Who would do something like this?" She glanced over at Marquis and Nieko, knowing that they would be watching Rain's reaction as well. "I mean, really," Amber continued, this time shaking her head. "Who in the world would do something this tragic? And why?"

Rain, sniffling a bit, looked away. It was almost as if she hadn't heard Amber ask the question. Instantly, Amber, Marquis, and Nieko felt even more suspicious than they had felt before. Rain looked back down at Amber. "Can we at least go and see him if we want to?" she asked.

Amber looked into Rain's eyes with cold, stone eyes. She shrugged. "Sure," she said. "It's terrible that you had to be there for all of this. I am happy, at least, that you ain't get hurt. I heard about it all, and remember what you was sayin' last night. You are so lucky that none of that happened to you."

"Yeah," Rain said, looking down toward the carpet as if she were lost in thought. "Lucky." She paused. "Excuse me."

Rain walked away and quickly pranced toward the hallway. Once she'd gotten far enough away from the waiting area, Amber looked at Marquis and Nieko with slanted eyes. "You see that?" she asked.

The two young men nodded. "Hmm, hmm," Nieko said. "Somethin' is up with that chick. Somethin' about her just don't sit well with me."

"What is really messed up is how she act like she don't even remember us," Marquis said. "That's messed up. We done met that chick like how many times, Nieko?"

"Like two or three times," Nieko answered. "She should know who we are."

Amber nodded. "I wonder if that little bitch had somethin' to do with my son windin' up in a hospital and maybe havin' injuries that are gonna affect him for the rest of his life," she said. "I really wonder."

Without speaking, Marquis jumped up and headed toward the hallway. Amber and Nieko looked at one another, each wondering where he was going. And why.

Rain walked up to Lamarcus' room and cautiously turned and entered. She stepped up to the side of the bed. Now, nearly a day later, in the bright hospital rooms, she got a better look at Lamarcus' face. It was catastrophic, to say the least. Rain couldn't help but put her hand up to her mouth and shake her head. She'd never seen anyone take such a beating and live to see tomorrow.

"Why they go so hard?" she asked, softly. "They ain't have to try to kill him like this. They ain't have to do this at all. This was just too much."

Little did Rain know, as she was crying into her palms and wondering why Qoree and his boys had gone so far, Marquis was standing outside of the doorway. He could hear word for word what Rain said. Before she'd even had the chance to leave the room, he rushed back to the waiting area.

Just as Rain turned around to head back out into the lobby, her phone vibrated in her pocket. She pulled it out and saw that it was a number she didn't know. And she knew exactly what that meant. "Hello?" she answered, feeling her heart beat faster.

"You at the hospital still?" a man asked.

"Yeah," Rain answered. "I'm about to leave."

"Okay," the man said. "Come right here, okay. Come right over here."

"Okay, I'm on my way," Rain said. "And—"

Before Rain could finish the sentence, the line had cut off. She looked back at Lamarcus, so many emotions coming over her. "I'm so sorry," she said, touching his bruised arm as she looked at the different machines hooked into his body. "I'm so sorry, Lamarcus. I had to. I had to."

Rain stormed out of the hospital room. There was no way she could look into Lamarcus' mother's eyes again. She went straight to the elevator doors and waited. Without looking over toward the waiting room, she got onto the elevator and headed back downstairs. Amber, having just heard from Marquis what he had heard when he stood outside of Lamarcus' hospital room, looked at Nieko then Marquis. "Hmm, hmm," she said, nodding her head. "Something about that chick, I swear. Danez might be on to something. Something about that little bitch just don't sit well with me. I remember when I was young and stuff and I knew her type. The type you just can't trust, especially if you got money."

Nieko nodded, knowing that he'd seen some fine women play some horrible games on dudes in the hoods of New York before coming to Indianapolis. "Let me call Danez," he said. "I think he need to know what we just found out, and that Lamarcus's little chick went rushing out without saying goodbye or nothin'. That definitely don't seem right."

***

Qoree smiled wildly when he hung up from talking to Rain. Not only did he feel accomplished in the fact that he had put one of his rivals into the hospital for coming onto his territory without permission, but he also liked having an inside informant – a person close to the situation that nobody would ever suspect, or so he thought.

Qoree pulled his blunt back up to his lips as he turned back to the show before him. He sat in his house, in his basement family room, watching a chick that went by the name Chocolate Bunny, although her real name was Lala, twerk. The five-foot, 140 pound chick had an ass that was out of this world – an ass that would even give Nicki Minaj a run for her money. And she could make it clap nonstop, driving Qoree crazy.

"Damn, you got a fat ass!" Qoree exclaimed after watching Chocolate Bunny make it clap in perfect rhythm for several seconds nonstop.

The chocolate-colored girl, who was known for not only her ass but also for her Asian-like eyes, looked back at Qoree. "You like that shit, nigga?" she asked.

Like an excited kid, Qoree nodded and smiled. "Bring that ass over here," he said, leaning forward on the couch. "Bring that ass over here right now so a nigga can put his face in it."

Doing just as she'd been told, Chocolate Bunny backed up toward the leather couch. Once she was close enough to push her ass into Qoree's face, she bent over and made her ass jiggle. This drove Qoree crazy, causing his rock hard manhood to tent in his red sweatpants. She then felt Qoree lean in and press his face between her ass cheeks. This only motivated Chocolate Bunny even more to make her ass jiggle even harder. Following the beat to a Sauce Walka song, Chocolate Bunny clapped her ass so hard the cheeks moved separate from one another. They slapped the sides of Qoree's face, which was wedged deep in.

Not being able to hold back anymore, Qoree grabbed Chocolate Bunny's hips and turned her around. Aggressively, he tossed her onto the couch, causing her to giggle. He then turned her over onto her back, watching how her thighs and ass jiggled with

64

any movement her body made. He then pried her legs apart and pushed his face down between her legs. Right away, Chocolate Bunny felt Qoree's tongue ravishing her pussy. This was so much so that she squealed and fidgeted about, rubbing the top of Qoree's head as he flicked his tongue back and forth against her clit.

Qoree went on lavishing Chocolate Bunny's pussy. Instead of feeling ready to have sex and bless her with long, deep strokes, he just kept thinking that he needed to talk to Rain. He needed to know the impact of last night. And he hadn't even gotten around to counting the money he'd taken from Lamarcus' house last night. His eyes would nearly pop out of his head at the thought of sitting by a money machine and counting the money. He thanked God for blessing him with knowing Rain, as she'd proven to be the perfect connection.

"We gotta stop," Qoree said, pulling his head up. "We gon' have to finish this later, baby."

"Damn," Chocolate Bunny said, gently kicking her legs. "Why, Baby? Why Qoree?"

"'Cause," Qoree said, "you know I gotta see that Rain chick when she come through. She gon' be on her way soon and I can't have her walk in and see a nigga with his head in your pussy."

"Shit, Qoree," Chocolate Bunny said, standing up. She put her hand on her hip and looked at Qoree. "Why you get me warmed up like this if you wasn't gonna finish what you started?"

Qoree, always turned on when Chocolate Bunny would stand up and act like a strong woman to him, quickly jumped up and slapped her big, chocolate ass. He watched it ripple and snickered. "You betta calm that ass down before I fuck that pussy up for real later on," Qoree said. "Just go on to the bedroom and I'll be back there in a little bit. You know I'm deep in this shit with them niggas that came into The Land without talkin' to me. You know what? Calm that pussy down for a minute and you can help me count all that money. How you like that?"

Chocolate Bunny smiled and scurried along, quickly rushing back to the bedroom. Qoree shook his head as he watched her ass jiggle with each step she took until she disappeared. "Damn, that chick got a ass on her," he said to himself. "That shit don't make no sense."

Qoree finished getting dressed. Not soon after he slid his shirt over his head, he heard a light tap at his door. Grabbing his pistol out of the drawer in the end table on the left side of the couch, he stepped up to the door and looked out. It was Rain. She knocked again, ever so softly as if she was knocking to not be heard. Quickly, Qoree opened the door and told Rain to come in. Once she'd stepped inside, he looked out into his front yard and looked around before closing the door.

"Ain't nobody follow me if that is what you was worried about," Rain said.

"Don't worry about what I'm worried about," Qoree said, closing the door. "This is my house and if I wanna look outside, I am." He paused and looked Rain up and down. Even though she really wasn't that attractive of a woman, he had learned over at Lamarcus' house that she was certainly a good actress. "Well, well , well," he said, shaking his head. "Ain't you quite the actress. They talk about the Oscars being so white. They should put you in a movie playing the crying, whining woman and you would clean up real nice."

Rain slid out of her jacket and flipped her hair back. "Qoree, that's not funny," she said. "You should see him. You coulda got him killed. What did you go so hard for? I mean, really. Damn. You ain't have to make it like some big shootout in a movie or somethin' like that. Shit, you almost got me killed."

"Calm the fuck down," Qoree said, going back over to the couch. "You know we wasn't gon' shoot you. I told you how it was gon' work. We was gon shoot at the upper corners of the window where the nigga wouldn't even be tall enough to get hit by a fuckin' bullet. You know I ain't wanna kill the nigga. Shit, I'm done gettin' bodies on me. Them days is through. Plus, I just wanted to prove a point. Like you said, the nigga ain't dead."

"Yeah, whatever," Rain said. She turned and looked at Qoree. "So?" she said.

"So, what?" Qoree asked. "What the fuck you say so for?"

"When the fuck do I get my money?" Rain asked. "I mean, you did go and get the money while I was fuckin' knocked out, didn't you? I mean, that was part of the fuckin' plan. I mean, getting the money was. I don't know where the fuck that knocking me out part came from. I don't remember us even talking about that shit."

Qoree chuckled. "We talked about it," he said. "You just wasn't there to hear us when we was talkin' about it. I meant to tell you, but shit, you know a nigga gets busy and stuff. You'll be all right. You gon' get your money when we through with this shit, okay? You ain't forgot that we gotta get the other nigga, did you?"

"No," Rain said, almost wishing she'd never gotten involved. "I ain't forgot about that shit. That nigga Danez was up at the hospital. Shit, he was the one who took me and Lamarcus to the fuckin' hospital."

"Good," Qoree said. "At least that show that that nigga got some fuckin' respect for somebody. 'Cause he sure ain't show me no respect."

"So, how long are you gon' fuckin' draw this out?" Rain asked. "I mean, how long am I gon' have to wait to get my money?"

"Bitch, would you stop actin' thirsty for a minute, would you?" Qoree asked. "I mean, you did a real good job playin' the damsel in distress over there and shit. And you been doin' real good keepin' close to him without tellin' him. You remember what I told you would happen if you said a word to him about this shit, don't you?"

Rain turned around quickly. "Yes, nigga, I do," she answered, feeling ashamed. "I remember. You ain't go after my grandmother, did you?"

"No," Qoree said. "You know you ain't gotta worry about me goin' after Granny if you just play along. You play along and don't nobody on your side even get hurt. It's really just that easy, you feel me? Just keep playin' along until we get both niggas. Your grandma goes untouched in her little assisted living place, and I get the point across not only to a couple niggas that overstepped they boundaries, but also the other niggas that stay over in The Land. I'm about to start movin' more work and shit. Plus, there's gon' be some businesses in the area that I'mma have to have little meetings with to let them know how stuff works in the area – let them know that they can't just make money off my niggas without payin' me a little neighborhood fee."

Rain pressed her lips together, hating that she'd even gotten mixed up in this situation. Just as she was realizing how much she liked Lamarcus, Qoree came walking into her life. And when he did, he already had information and a plan – information from which a source was never told to her. All Rain knew was that if she didn't cooperate, her 86-year-old grandmother, who lived in an assisted living facility on the north side of Indianapolis, would suddenly disappear. Rain would never be able to live with herself if she knew that something happened to her grandmother. For that reason, she had to choose to go along, even if it meant that Lamarcus could wind up with life-threatening and life-changing injuries.

"So, what's next?" Rain asked Qoree. "I mean, can I at least know that, or am I gon' have to live my life on fuckin' edge for the next six months?"

Qoree liked how Rain was so upfront. In many ways she was tough, but life had her by the balls, so to speak. Therefore, her disposition was somewhat weak. Qoree stood up and went to get himself a beer out of the refrigerator. "Tell me about what the fuck happened at the hospital," he demanded. "You ain't even told me that shit yet. I told you that you gotta tell me every fuckin' thing you know, from when the nigga Lamarcus is at home to when he got people around and who. You still ain't found out where that nigga Danez live, have you?"

"No," Rain answered. "All I know is that the nigga live downtown, but I ain't wanna push too hard about that with Lamarcus because what the fuck is a nigga gon' think of his chick try'na find out where his dude lives. That don't even sound right. And he don't talk about it much. All I know it that the nigga and his girl Ronnisha live downtown."

"Yeah, I remember you saying that," Qoree said. "I asked around, but don't nobody know this Ronnisha chick. She must not be out in the streets all that much and stuff. Anyway, you still ain't sayin' what the fuck happened up at the hospital."

"Well, basically," Rain began, walking over to the counter and propping herself up onto a bar stool, "Lamarcus is hooked up on all these machines. He look like he got hit by a couple of buses up on the interstate then ran over a couple of times. I don't even know if he's breathing on his own, but I ain't wanna ask.

"When I was just up there just now, his mother was there and so was two other niggas up there that I mighta seen once or twice, but I really don't know them. Them niggas was definitely actin' funny, but I ain't think nothin' of it. Danez wasn't there, but I'm sure he'd been up there earlier or something."

"Actin' funny?" Qoree asked. "What you mean they was up there actin' funny? What the fuck do that mean?"

"Damn, nigga," Rain said. "I mean, them niggas was up there actin' funny. Simple as that. It was like they was lookin' at me crazy and shit."

In one swift move, the entire mood in Qoree's house changed. Almost as if he had been planning it, Qoree pulled a knife out of his kitchen drawer and held it up to Rain's neck. Immediately, she broke a sweat. "Why?" she asked, holding her head up and looking into Qoree's eyes. "Why the fuck are you doin' this?" She shook uncontrollably, as this was the first time in her life she'd ever had a knife to her neck.

CHAPTER 8

Ronnisha drove home as quickly as she could without getting pulled over by the police. She couldn't believe that going to her niece's birthday party would wind up being one of the worst things she'd done in recent years. She hated how her family was always so against her. And the older she got, the more apparent it became that Brineesha was really the special one in the family. Throwing her father into the mix was really only the cherry on top.

"Fuck them niggas," Ronnisha said to herself as she waited at a red light in downtown Indianapolis. "Fuck my daddy, too. Who the fuck do he think he is to come walkin' into my life after not really seein' him for even a year straight and he think that he can tell me somethin' about my life and who I'm seein'?"

Ronnisha finished her journey to her apartment building. Upon entering the garage, she was pleased to see that Danez was indeed there. If there was one thing in the world that Ronnisha could count on, it would be Danez. He had never let her down, and he always had her back. She couldn't help but think back to the times where a dude would say the wrong thing or touch her inappropriately in the club and Danez would stand up for her. She watched many dudes take the fade from Danez for coming at her the wrong way. The very idea of him letting harm come to her, such as with what her family was suggesting, just didn't even make sense.

Ronnisha, still watching her back, headed up to her apartment. By the time she'd gotten to their floor and had let herself in, she felt a lot better. The hallways seemed clear, as was the parking garage. Inside, Ronnisha was greeted by Danez. He sat on the couch, with the television on and smoking a blunt. It was very obvious to her that he was feeling some type of way. She always knew when he was upset about something.

"Hey, Baby," Danez said.

Ronnisha quickly slid out of her coat and threw it over the back of a chair. She rushed over to Danez and hugged him. "So, what happened?" she asked. "What was goin' on up at the hospital when you left?"

"Shit, his mama was there," Danez said. "The doctor came out with some real bad, fucked up news." He shook his head. "I don't fuckin' believe this shit."

Danez took the next few minutes to explain everything that Doctor Adair had said about Lamarcus' surgeries. His nerves had been affected and could cause lifetime damage if the surgeries weren't able to fix them. Instantly, Ronnisha felt horrible. "You can't be serious?" she said.

Danez looked at his baby. "Do I look like I'm playin?" he asked. "I mean, really. That shit was so fucked up. The look on Miss Amber face nearly broke my heart."

Just as Ronnisha was about to ask about the Rain chick, Danez's phone went off. He pulled it out of his jacket pocket and saw that it was Marquis calling. "Hold up," he said. "It's Marquis callin'. Him and Nieko was comin' up to the hospital right when I was leavin' and shit." He held the phone up to the side of his head. "Yeah, wassup?"

"Nigga, where you at?" Marquis asked.

"Shit, at home," Danez answered. "Ronnisha just walked in the door and I was talkin' to her and shit. Wassup? Y'all niggas still up at the hospital or what?"

"Yeah, but we 'bout to leave," Marquis answered. "Lamarcus' mama is real tired. But, nigga, that ain't what I called to tell you about. That chick Rain came back up here again."

Danez looked at Ronnisha and whispered Rain's name. "What about her?" he asked Marquis. "What she say?"

"Man, that bitch is fake as a fuckin' three dollar bill," Marquis said. "I had a fucked up feelin' about her. So did Nieko. And you already know how Miss Amber don't play. She looked at that bitch with all kinds of shade and shit. I think you was right. I think she mighta had something to do with this shit."

"What I tell you, nigga?" Danez asked. "What I tell you? Nigga, we need to go over to Lamarcus' place and see what the fuck is up."

"I feel you on that," Marquis said. "When you try'na go and shit? We up for it. Me and Nieko."

Danez looked at Ronnisha before delving back into the conversation. "Bet," he said. "Why don't y'all head over here right now and we can go from there?"

71

Marquis agreed, telling Danez that he and Nieko were on their way downtown. When Danez hung up, he could look at Ronnisha and tell by the look on her face that she wanted every detail possible.

"That Rain chick was just up there," Danez said. "And he said she look shady as fuck."

"But what would she have to gain by doin' some shit like this?" Ronnisha asked. "I mean, I don't know the chick and stuff, but I'm really try'na think what she would have to gain by having the house shot up and shit. I mean, wasn't she over there too when it all happened? Ain't that what you said?"

Danez nodded. "Yeah," he answered. "She was knocked the fuck out on the couch when I first walked in the door. But you never know, especially nowadays. For all we know, there could be something goin' on behind the scenes for her that make it good for her to set up Lamarcus, even if her own life is almost at risk."

Within fifteen minutes, the doorman downstairs had called up to their apartment and let them know that a Marquis and Nieko had arrived and were waiting to be allowed to come up. Once they'd gotten to the door, Danez quickly opened it. They shook hands and hugged.

"Lamarcus ain't wake up yet, did he?" Danez asked.

Nieko and Marquis slid out of their jackets and threw them over the back of chairs. "Naw," Nieko said. "That nigga is still pretty fucked up."

"What was that chick Rain saying?" Ronnisha asked. "I mean, what make y'all think that she had something to do with this. I just wanna know in case y'all need me to talk to her and see if I can read her. You know how I am when it comes to females. I can talk to any of them and see right through them and see what they really about."

"I feel you on that," Marquis said. He followed Nieko as the two of them crossed the living room and plopped down onto a couch. "Basically, what had happened was she went to Lamarcus' room and shit after she came over and spoke to us and Amber. I waited for her to go into the room then I went and stood just outside of the door and heard what she said."

"What she said?" Danez asked. "What the fuck you mean what she said? How the fuck she gon' be sayin' somethin' to a nigga who beat up so fuckin' bad he practically almost in a damn coma?"

"Exactly," Marquis said. "So, like I was sayin', I was standing outside of the door when I heard her talking about how sorry she was and how she didn't mean for it all to go that far and all that."

"She didn't mean for it to go that far?" Danez said, now pacing around the middle of the living room floor.

Ronnisha could feel the anger and resentment coming off of Danez. The vibes were just too strong to ignore. She quickly stood up and stepped over to him, putting her hands on his shoulders. "Calm down, Danez," she said in a comforting way. "Just calm down, Baby."

"Don't tell me to calm down," Danez said. "I knew something was up with that bitch, and now I know that she set this shit up. I should go up to the hospital and wait on that bitch and fuck her up right then and there, on sight."

"No," Nieko said. "Don't do no shit like that. You heard about them niggas up in Ft. Wayne who went up in a hospital to get some nigga back. Them white people up there wound up givin' him and his friends like life in prison and shit. Don't do that. Not at the hospital. Plus, you know Miss Amber is there. And even if this chick was involved with what happened with her son, she not gon' sit back and watch some man jump on another woman and be okay with it."

Danez took a deep breath before coming to his senses. He thanked Ronnisha for just being her then looked at his boys. "Bet," he said. "Come on, niggas. We need to go to that house and see what the fuck that nigga Qoree might have been after. Was it something that Lamarcus had in there and he got in the way or was it Lamarcus himself or both. I wanna fuckin' know so I can know how fuckin' bad we need to torture this nigga when we do finally catch up to him."

Danez slipped back into his coat as Nieko and Marquis did the same. Ronnisha then stood up and went for her jacket. "Where you goin'?" Danez asked, looking at Ronnisha.

"What you mean where am I goin'?" Ronnisha asked. "You just said that we was goin' up to Lamarcus's house to see what the fuck mighta went down there."

"Baby, yeah, but…" Danez said, hesitantly. "You know I can't have you possibly getting' caught up in this shit."

"It's too late," Ronnisha said, confidently. "And you can't tell me what you will and won't have me do, Danez. I'mma go with y'all, okay. I can sit and be the watch person in case the police roll by or somethin' look funny while y'all up in the house."

Danez looked at his boys and smiled. "Okay," he said. "I guess you supposed to be a bad chick now, huh?"

Ronnisha smiled and grabbed her purse. She threw it over her shoulder then walked right between Danez and Marquis and Nieko. She opened the door and looked back at Danez. "I was a bad chick the day you met me," she said. "I guess ain't nobody told you."

Just then, Nieko and Marquis snickered at Danez, who hung his head low because of the humor of it all. The three men then followed Ronnisha to the elevator and down to Danez's Ford Explorer. They climbed in and quickly left the garage.
***

As usual, Lamarcus' street was quiet and dark. The canopy of trees crawling over the top of the street made the neighborhood seem all the more darker. Ronnisha, who was sitting in the back seat, looked out at the nice, brick, ranch-style homes on either side of the street. She couldn't help but think about how one day, she hoped to have one of these houses. With the kind of money that Danez was starting to make out in the streets, and how he was being smart about keeping his businesses up and growing, she knew that sooner or later, they would be living the good life – she knew that they would be living in an even better place than they lived right now downtown.

Danez pulled up to Lamarcus' house and looked up. Hearing about what had gone down was one thing. Seeing the result of such was completely another. When he came to a stop, all four of them looked up the driveway.

"You gon' pull up in the driveway or what?" Ronnisha asked.

Danez looked over at Marquis, who was sitting in the front passenger seat. "What you think?" he asked. "I mean, we can pull up in the driveway and shit, but if the police ride by and they already know what the fuck happened here, then they probably gon' find it funny that there is somebody parked up in the driveway and shit,

74

especially in the middle of the night like this." He looked down at the time, seeing that 11 o'clock was quickly approaching.

Marquis shrugged. "I mean," he said, "I think we betta off parkin' up there." He pointed at the wooded area on the other side of the property. "At least if we park up there, people might think that we in the house across the street or somethin'. I remember Lamarcus sayin' that some of these houses is empty and have been since the fuckin' economy went down, but I don't know which one."

Danez looked up and down the street. "Yeah, I don't know which ones either," he said.

"He right, he right," Ronnisha said, feeling anxious. "Just pull up there and park. And, you know what, that's even better because I can still see the house and shit from the street and with the trees and stuff right there, it's gon be even darker so we ain't gotta worry about nobody ridin' by and seein' me."

Danez liked the idea, so he pulled up just beyond where the property ended. He parked in the shadows of the wooded area and turned the car off. After a few quiet moments, he was ready to go. He looked up and down the street, thinking that nobody was really watching.

"Okay," Danez said. "We gon' go in here and see what the fuck is up. I wanna know if Qoree got Lamarcus' money and shit or if he just came to fuck him up and leave. If this nigga took the money, we know we got a fuckin' problem cause we worked hard as fuck for that money and can't let that nigga just keep it like that without huntin' him down and shit."

The three men climbed out of the SUV. Ronnisha quickly scooted over to the left side, where the window had already been lowered a bit. Danez, waiting for Marquis and Nieko to head up toward the house, leaned in. "You sure you gon' be okay out here?" he asked.

Ronnisha smiled and slid the handle of her pistol out of her purse. "Yeah," she said. "I think I'll be alright. Y'all just be careful. And make sure that you don't turn on no lights, okay. Especially since it look like the fuckin' windows is blown out and stuff."

"Okay," Danez said. "And you lay low out here, so don't nobody think that nobody else is sittin' in here. You got your phone with you, right?"

"You know I do," Ronnisha said, sliding her iPhone out of her pocket. "Just make sure that if I call you, you fuckin' answer, okay?"

"Okay," Danez said. On that note, he quickly kissed Ronnisha then hurried across the wooded front yard and into the house.

Danez approached the front door, just like Nieko and Marquis. As they were trying to pick the lock, Danez stopped them. "Naw, naw," he said. "We need to go in through the back and shit so these nosey ass white people that might be lookin' won't see shit. At least in the back, we can kick the fuckin' door in if we want. You know how these kinds of neighborhoods are. After the police been up here and stuff, they suddenly see the fuckin' house that prolly nobody paid attention to before."

Agreeing, Marquis and Nieko followed Danez around to the back of the beige, stone house. All they could do when passing by the blown out windows was shake their heads. It looked as if a war had broken out on the property. Everything about it let them know that Qoree was very serious about getting what he wanted, be it the money or be it Lamarcus.

Walking closely along the side of the house, the three men walked in a single file line around to the back door. There, Danez looked around before relaxing. The back end of the property was so wooded that he no longer felt the anxiety of breaking and entering. "Watch out," he said then stepped back. He kicked the door open and the three men stepped inside of the kitchen.

Within a matter of seconds, they were out in the family room – the very room where clearly most of the beating, if not all, had gone down. While the rooms were dark, there was enough light coming in through the windows from the moonlight and couple of nearby streetlights for them to see the streaks of blood on the carpet.

"Yeah," Danez said, seeing the look of disgust on his boys' faces. "This shit was bad when I got here." He pointed at the floor, just in front of the couch. "This is where I found him when I got here, but I could tell that some shit went down on the pool table. Look."

Just then, their eyes followed the smears of blood as they went into the back room. Marquis and Nieko stepped into the room and saw the broken pool stick, as well as the huge blotches of blood on the green of the pool table. All they could do was shake their heads as they felt their own anger building inside. They then came back to join Danez.

"Yeah," Nieko said, nodding. "I don't give a fuck if that nigga got any money or not. We gon' go after that nigga for doin' this shit. And that bitch, Rain, since she had somethin' to do with that shit."

Danez then noticed that the basement door was slightly ajar. "Look," he said, pointing. "I know the police and shtick probably went down there to see what the fuck was up. You know how they always try'na look for any and everything that they can."

Danez led Nieko and Marquis down the dark basement stairwell. At first, Nieko had turned a light on, flipping the switch on the wall out of instinct.

"Nigga, what the fuck?" Danez said, looking back and up the stairs. "This basement got windows and shit that look out at the front yard and shit. What the fuck is you doin'?"

Nieko quickly turned the light out as they went the rest of the way down the stairs. They then pulled out their cell phones as they looked around. Here, they were not as familiar with their surroundings. Sure, they'd each been over to Lamarcus' house on several occasions, however the basement generally wasn't where the entertaining took place, even though it was built for that. And the few times they'd been in the basement were brief, so they really didn't know their way around.

Out in Danez's SUV, Ronnisha kept her head low. She noticed when the basement light had popped on, causing her eyes to bulge. Immediately, she looked up and down the block as she pulled her phone out. Just as she was about to call inside and tell Danez to turn the light off because of how much it stuck out on the dark property, the light went off.

"Whew," Ronnisha said, feeling herself get a little nervous. She then went back to being the lookout. A few minutes passed and she saw something that sent fear and anxiety riveting through her body: a police car had turned at the corner to the south and was slowly headed up the block.

"Shit, shit, shit," Ronnisha said, sliding down onto the floor. "This would fuckin' happen when we here. Fuck. I knew some shit like this…"

Realizing that she needed to act quickly in letting Danez know, she put her head as low to the floor as she could without twisting her body into painful positions. She called Danez. "Answer the phone, Danez," she said, wishing that she could peek up and see how close the police car was to Danez's SUV. The only bright side to this, if there was one, was the fact that the officer hadn't turned his lights on just yet.

"Yeah?" Danez answered. "Wassup, Baby? Is everything okay out there?"

"No, it's not," Ronnisha said, talking quietly. "Y'all niggas betta not turn no lights on or come walkin' out the house just yet. There is a fuckin' police car ridin' down the block."

"What?" Danez said. "A police car? Fuck! Where is it now? Where did it go? It is still ridin' down the block?"

"Hold up," Ronnisha said. "I gotta look."

"But, Baby…" Danez said.

His words trailed off as Ronnisha slowly lifting her head up. She looked out the back of the SUV and saw that the police car was indeed slowing down in front of Lamarcus' house. "Watch out, y'all," she said to Danez, cutting him off as he was telling her to be careful and make sure that she stayed unseen. "The police car is slowin' down out front." She then paused and watched as the police car increased speed and went on up the block. "Okay," she said. "Y'all coo now. He pulled off and stuff. I don't think he was really lookin'. He was just ridin' around. Hurry up so we can get the hell outta here, okay, Danez?"

"Okay," Danez said. "We'll be out there in a minute."

Ronnisha hung up the phone, hoping to God that tonight didn't go the wrong way – something that could happen at any minute. The only thing worse, at least in her mind, that could happen would be Qoree riding by. She didn't even know the guy that well, but he sure seemed far more ruthless than any police officer would be.

Danez slid his phone back into his pocket. "The cop pulled off," he said to Marquis and Nieko, who were both alarmed. Nieko had served time in a prison in Connecticut before coming to Indiana, so he was extra cautious when it came to dealing with the police. Marquis, on the other hand, was still on papers – still having to visit a probation officer at a moment's notice. For him to be found in this

78

house, especially in this kind of situation, would be a surefire way to wind up back in prison.

Danez, on a mission to get out of the house quickly, walked ahead with his cell phone acting as light. They came to the basement's spare room where there was a bed. Upon stepping inside and shining the light around the room, they all stopped when the light landed on the corner to the left of the door – the corner where the bookshelf had been moved. The safe was out in the open, it's door hanging open.

"Shit," Danez said, as the three of them rushed over to the safe. Nieko and Marquis watched as Danez stuck his hand inside and felt around. Danez then stood up, with flared nostrils. "That nigga Qoree robbed Lamarcus. He robbed the nigga blind as fuck."

"What?" Marquis asked. "Ain't shit in there? Nothin'?"

Danez pointed at the safe and said, "Feel around for yourself, nigga. He got all of the fuckin' money. And I ain't try'na count my boy's coins and shit, but I know he had at least a hundred stacks in there. You know how Lamarcus was with his money."

Marquis felt around inside of the safe then Nieko did the same. When the two men stood up, all they could do was look around in confusion. "Hold up," Nieko said. "You don't think that Lamarcus would have had all his money just in this one place?"

Danez shrugged. "Shit, I don't know," he said. "But if he did, we need to hurry up and figure that out before another cop come ridin' down the street."

The three men rushed back up to the main floor of the house and quickly searched through the three bedrooms. They found nothing. With this in mind, they looked out at the front yard to be sure it was safe to head back out to Danez's SUV. They then rushed back out of the back door, around the side of the house, then across the wooded front yard in the dark of the night.

Ronnisha, seeing that Danez, Marquis, and Nieko were coming back toward the SUV, quickly reached up front and unlocked the door. They then jumped inside, Danez started the engine, and they pulled off. "Yeah, that nigga got Lamarcus good," Danez said, rushing to the corner then turning to get to the nearest busy street. "That nigga Qoree got Lamarcus good. This shit is fucked up."

"What?" Ronnisha asked. "What did y'all find?"

"It ain't what we found," Danez said, shaking his head. "It's what we ain't find. Ain't a damn thing in that safe. This was a fuckin' setup. And I think that trick Rain was in on it." He paused. "No, I know she was in on it."

Ronnisha turned and looked out of the window at the street. Just then, she knew how serious things had gotten. And she knew that if they didn't play their cards right then the money that she and Danez had could be the very thing to bring them down – the very thing to make them a target.

CHAPTER 9

That night, Ronnisha and Danez went back to their apartment downtown. There, because they had to work the next day, Marquis and Nieko left. However, before they left, they each tried to guess how much money Lamarcus may have had in his safe before Qoree shot his way into his house. After some discussion, they came to the conclusion that it could very well have been $100,000, but they didn't know the exact number. When Danez laid his head down to go to sleep, he was obviously tired. More than being tired, though, Ronnisha could see that he was agitated. Careful about how she approached the topic, she insisted that they talk a little bit before Danez went to sleep. He rolled over and expressed himself, and his anger. And it all told Ronnisha that this would probably be the toughest, and riskiest, situation of his entire life. When Ronnisha went to sleep with Danez's arms around her, just before he fell asleep, he told her that he loved her. Ronnisha, with her eyes open and looking at the blinds over the window on the other side of the room, spoke softly and let Danez know, "Baby, I'm down for you, until the end. I'mma help you with this, no matter what you say." Danez smiled and hugged Ronnisha even tighter before finally falling asleep.

The next morning – Thursday morning – Ronnisha was the first to wake up. She wasn't particularly tired, but she didn't feel well rested. She smiled, as the sunlight seeped through the blinds and into their bedroom, and looked down at Danez's strong arms and how they were still wrapped around her. She always felt so safe in his arms, almost to the point that there was no place she'd rather be.

Just as Ronnisha was turning over to look into Danez's sleeping face, as she often did when she woke up before him, she heard vibrating. After grabbing her phone, which sat on the nightstand on her side of the bed, she figured out that it was Danez's phone ringing. She pushed his shoulder, pushing him out of his deep sleep.

"What? What?" Danez said, waking up quickly. Much of his night was not deep sleep, because he knew he'd have to watch his back closely from now on, or at least until they caught up with Qoree and his goons. "What's wrong?"

"The phone," Ronnisha said, pointing to Danez's side of the bed. "Your phone is ringing, Baby. Your phone is ringing."

81

"Oh shit," Danez said, pulling his arms from around Ronnisha. He turned over and reached down to his pile of clothes on the floor next to the bed. When he came back up with his phone, he and Ronnisha looked into the screen at the same time. Danez looked at Ronnisha when they saw that it was Lamarcus' mother, Amber, calling. It was about 9:30, so it was rather early.

"Answer, answer," Ronnisha said.

"Hello?" Danez said, running his hand over his face. "Hello?"

"Hey, Danez," Amber said. "I didn't wake you up, did I?"

"Naw, Miss Amber," Danez answered. "You didn't wake me up. I was actually just wakin' up to go ahead and get my day goin' and stuff. Wassup? What's goin' on, Miss Amber?"

"Well, I was just callin' to tell you that the doctors just got done doin' one of the first surgeries," Amber said. "So, the main doctor, came out and told me that in a little bit, people will be able to talk to him and stuff. I didn't know if you was comin' up here today or not."

"Come on, Miss Amber," Danez said. "You know I'mma be up there today. Actually, I can come up there in a little bit to talk to Lamarcus if you don't mind."

"Of course," Amber said. "You know you can come up here whenever you want. I'm just watching out for that Rain chick."

"I heard she was up there last night," Danez said, looking over at Ronnisha.

"Yeah, she was," Amber said. "Hmm, hmm." She paused. "I don't trust that chick no further than I can throw her little prissy ass. Somethin' about her just seem like she up to no good. She don't seem like she real at all, to me."

"Yeah, I'll talk to you about that when I get up there," Danez said. "I ain't feelin' her either. Well, I can get up and goin' in a minute and me and Ronnisha gon' come up there." Danez looked at Ronnisha, waiting for her to shake her head to let him know that she agreed. "Yeah, me and Ronnisha gon' be up there in a little bit so we can see Lamarcus and stuff and talk to him. I know you happy he's waking up and stuff."

"Yes, I am," Amber said. "But we still got a long way to go, so we'll see. Okay, well I won't hold you up and stuff, Danez. I'll let you get moving. I'll see you up here."

Danez said goodbye then ended the phone call. He looked at Ronnisha, who had just opened her mouth to ask, "So, what she say?"

Danez yawned then answered, "She said that he just got done with the first surgery. She said that the doctor came out and told her that Lamarcus was going to be awoke in a little bit to talk and stuff if we wanted to come up there. I told her we would."

"Of course," Ronnisha said. "You know I'm down to go up there. You and Lamarcus been best friends for like forever and stuff. Shit, he's practically like a brother to you."

"Yeah," Danez said, nodding his head. "He really is. I mean... Well, nothing."

"No, what?" Ronnisha insisted. "Danez, you know I hate when you do that. I hate when you start a sentence or thought and don't finish it. Ain't nothin' in this world that you can't tell me, Danez. When you gonna understand that?"

"I ain't say I ain't understand that," Danez said, "but, anyway, I was thinkin' about somethin' last night when we got into bed and laid down and stuff. One, I was thinkin' about how mad I was gettin' by just imagining if Qoree and them niggas had killed my boy Lamarcus. I mean, what if one of them bullets had hit him or somethin'?"

"Don't think like that," Ronnisha said. "I mean, I know what you mean, but you really can't think like that. You will really worry yourself crazy if you just keep on thinkin' like that. All you really need to do is think about how that didn't happen and just be happy that it didn't."

"Yeah," Danez said, turning and looking at their bedroom ceiling. "I guess you right. You know how I be thinkin' the worst sometime."

"Yeah, well," Ronnisha said, laying her hand on his chest. "You can't think like that." She paused, taking a moment to put her head on his chest next to her hand. "So, you said *one*. That means that there is a number two and three or somethin'?"

"Yeah," Danez answered, hesitantly. "Last night, with you out in the truck while me and Marquis and Nieko was in the house."

"What about it?" Ronnisha asked. "Ain't nothin' happen or nothin' like that."

"Yeah, I know, Ronnisha," Danez said. "I know. But I was just thinkin' about how even when shit gets deep and dangerous, you still there for me. I ain't never had a chick like that. Most chicks just want money and shopping and stuff and they be gone."

Ronnisha lifted her head up and looked into Danez's face. She softly grabbed his chin and turned his head toward her side of the bed. "Danez, you ain't think that I was one of them up until last night, did you?" she asked, sounding concerned. "I mean, really. You ain't think that I was one of them here today but gone tomorrow-type chicks, did you?"

"Naw," Danez responded, shaking his head quickly. "You know I ain't think that. But, you know how shit can be sometime. Sometime you really don't know what somebody is about until shit get hard and stuff, that's all."

"Listen to me, Danez," Ronnisha said. "You know that I love you. And I am really here for you. I'm just as mad about what happened with Lamarcus as you are. I swear to God, I am. He is probably the one true friend you really got, then Marquis and Nieko, I guess. They cool dudes too."

"Yeah, they are," Danez said, nodding.

"And, just let me say this," Ronnisha said. "You need to know also that I'm here to help you catch up with this nigga Qoree or whatever you said his name is. I swear to God I am. And I put that on everything I love. I really do."

"Yeah, but," Danez said.

Quickly, Ronnisha put her finger over Danez's lips, signaling that he should be quiet. "No, let me talk," she said and smiled. "Just listen. Like I was sayin', I know that you worry about me and stuff, but ain't no chick out in these streets that's badder than me and you know it. You know that, Danez. I know you and I know you the kinda man that ain't gon' be wastin' his time on no weak ass, fake chicks. I'mma help you get with this Qoree nigga. In fact, I think you need me."

Danez smirked as Ronnisha moved her finger off of his lips. "Oh, is that right?" he asked, sarcastically. "How you think I need you? I wanna hear this shit."

"Okay," Ronnisha said, moving her neck side to side. "Well, you know that the Qoree dude already know who you are. I mean, everybody know who you are in The Land, so I don't think that he just went after Lamarcus by chance. So, I'm thinkin' that I can help because I'm a female."

"A female?" Danez said. "I mean, I know you a female, but what that gotta do with helpin' me with this?"

"'Cause," Ronnisha said. "I can get around and talk to people. You know how them niggas over in the hood talk and talk all day long. Ain't like they got shit else to do. I'mma get out and get to talkin', but not say too much. You know how I can get just about anyone to open up to me and practically tell me they life story."

"Yeah," Danez said. "You sure can. Remember when you was talkin' to my cousin Annie." He chuckled. "I remember when I took you around my family for the first time and we got back in the car and you started talking about all that shit Annie was out back tellin' you about the crazy ass life that she done had. I was like, *Okay, this chick can pull some real info outta niggas and stuff, without even tryin'*."

"Yeah, well, I can relate," Ronnisha said. "I mean, look at my family."

"I meant to ask you about how that shit with your family went," Danez said. "We ain't really get to talk about yesterday because I had to answer the phone and Marquis and Nieko came over and shit."

Ronnisha rolled her eyes. "No, not right now," she said. "I don't feel like talkin' about them niggas right now. As far as I'm concerned, I don't ever wanna see them niggas again in life. I ain't even thinkin' about none of them, except for my niece. In fact, if you want the truth, she the only reason I even go around them niggas. You know she love to see her auntie."

"Hmm, hmm," Danez said, wondering what had happened with Ronnisha's family. He put that topic to the side for the moment, knowing that he would return to it at a later time. "Shit," he said, stretching, "we better get going and stuff to get up to the hospital. You know I need to talk to Lamarcus."

"Well, wait a minute," Ronnisha said. "I mean, let his mama have a little bit of time with him so she can talk to her son and stuff without a buncha niggas up in her and his face, you know?"

"You right," Danez said, lowering his head back into his pillow. "Yeah, you right. We need to give them some space real quick."

"But, I know what we can do," Ronnisha said.

Before Danez could ask what, he felt Ronnisha's hand sliding down his stomach and onto his thigh. He smiled. "Oh, is that what you want?" he asked. "Is that what we can do?"

Ronnisha smiled. "That's the other thing," she said. "That's the other thing I was thinkin' I can help you with. You know you think better when you get up in this pussy."

Danez reached over Ronnisha's torso and slapped her fat, round ass. "Yeah, you right," he said, smiling. "That pussy is wet as fuck and always make me happy."

Ronnisha slowly lifted herself up until she was on both knees, one knee on either side of Danez's body. "And you know you like it in the morning," she said.

"Hmm, hmm," Danez said, with a big smile on his face. He nodded like a happy kid on Christmas day.

After Ronnisha leaned over and kissed Danez passionately, she scooted further down Danez's body until her head was level with his manhood. Danez quickly moved the sheet out of the way and looked down at Ronnisha. "You want some of that dick?" he asked.

Ronnisha giggled. Rather than answering, she pulled the head into her mouth.

"Fuck," Danez said and groaned. "That mouth feel good."

Ronnisha knew just how to get Danez to relax, which he clearly needed to do. She considered sucking on his manhood until it expanded from its soft, limp state to fully hard. She took as much into her mouth as she could before licking up and down the sides then his balls. All the while, Danez groaned. He eventually place the palm of his hand on the top of her head and rubbed it. "Damn, girl," he said. "You suck on that dick so good."

Ronnisha pleasured Danez orally for a few minutes more before she was ready to feel him inside of her. She lifted herself up and sat down on Danez's manhood. Danez, almost gone from the feeling, gripped Ronnisha's waist and helped her to lower all the way down his shaft, until all of his meat was inside of her.

"Fuck, Danez," Ronnisha said, her head turned up toward the ceiling. She planted her hands onto Danez's muscular chest, feeling the indentations of his tattoos. It took her a moment, as always, to get used to Danez's size. However, once she did, it was pure pleasure for the rest of the ride.

86

Danez gripped Ronnisha's hips as hard as he could, looking down at her thick thighs. "Fuck, you thick as fuck, girl," he said.

Ronnisha snickered. "Oh, this dick is big."

"That dick big, huh?" Danez asked, playfully. "You ready for that big dick to fuck this pussy up real quick."

Ronnisha took a deep breath and simply nodded her head. Before she knew it, Danez was lifting her body up and down his shaft. She loved how strong he was, and how he practically lifted her up effortlessly. As her insides slowly leaked with juices – juices that ran down Danez's shaft and caused his manhood to glaze over like ice – she went along with the motion. Within a few minutes, she was moaning and squealing as she rode him, enjoying every moment of it. And every inch.

Danez's face began to sweat as he breathed deeply and enjoyed some morning pussy. "Damn, this pussy feel good," he said. "Fuck." He bit his bottom lip.

Feeling her body become weak, Ronnisha simply couldn't take anymore. She was filled up to the max, as well as stretched, and could feel herself getting close to having an orgasm as she slid up and down on Danez's shaft. Not being able to control herself anymore, and breathing so heavily that one would think she was struggling for air, she collapsed. Her head was now lying on Danez's chest and he had slid his arms up to her back. He held her body close to his – chest to chest – as he pummeled her unmercifully.

"Fuck this pussy, Danez," Ronnisha screamed. "Damn, nigga. Shit this dick feel good." She then lifted her head up and they kissed passionately. She opened her eyes and looked into his determined face as he kept up the steady, and hard, pace. "I love you, Danez."

"I love you, too," Danez said. He then kissed her briefly. "I swear, Ronnisha. I love you, too."

Danez held Ronnisha tightly as he continued to dig deep into her.

"Fuck, I'm cumming, Danez!" Ronnisha announced, feeling her legs shake. "I'm cumming!"

Danez cracked a smile, as he knew he'd always been just what Ronnisha needed. "Cum on this dick," he told her, in a deep, heavy voice. "There you go, Baby. Just come on this dick."

87

Ronnisha's eyes rolled into the back of her head as she had an orgasm so powerful that she knew if she were to lift up off of Danez's manhood, she would squirt everywhere. He was the first man she'd been with to really get that kind of reaction out of her, and she loved every minute of it. As she'd often think to herself after sex, Danez had a big dick and knew how to use it.

"I'm 'bout to drop these kids off inside you, okay?" Danez asked, not really waiting for an answer. "Hold on."

In the thrall of aftershocks from her orgasm, Ronnisha lay her head on Danez's chest as he held her as close as possible to his body. With his legs bent up – knees in the air – Danez sped up. He stroked as hard as he could, and went balls deep with each thrust. His breathing increased as beads of sweat poured out of his head. "Shit!" he said. "Fuuuuuck."

Danez stopped, not being able to go on anymore. His body went limp as he and Ronnisha breathed in unison. Ronnisha's forehead was sweaty. Portions of her hair stuck to it, which she moved to the side. A few moments passed and she rolled off of him, lying on her side of the bed once again.

"That was all your fault," Danez said. "Look what you made me do."

"What I made you do?" Ronnisha asked, picking up on Danez's sarcasm. "Nigga, please." She giggled. "You know you love this pussy."

Danez chuckled and slapped Ronnisha's ass. "Yeah," he said, nodding. "You know I do. But next time I hit that pussy, I wanna hit that shit from the back. I swear, you musta had too much cake to eat at your niece's birthday party 'cause I feel like that ass is gettin' fatter."

"Boy, stop," Ronnisha said, playfully slapping Danez's chest. "You know my ass ain't gettin' no bigger. You just sayin' that. You always talkin' about my ass."

Danez chuckled as he rolled over and pulled himself out of the bed. Feeling heavy from having released a pretty big load, as well as a lot of pent-up energy, he stretched then looked at Ronnisha. "Come on," he said. "We better get goin' so we can get up to the hospital. I need to talk to my boy and see exactly what happened since the Rain chick was knocked out during all this, or so she say. I

88

wouldn't be surprised if she was pretending to be asleep when I came in the house, but that's another story."

Ronnisha got up and joined Danez in the shower. They showered together, kissing every so often as Ronnisha played with Danez's soft, dangling manhood. When they finished and climbed out of the shower, they put lotion on and got dressed. They slid into their jackets, Ronnisha grabbed her purse, and they headed to the hospital. Upon pulling into the garage in Danez's SUV, Danez parked. He stopped Ronnisha just as she was pushing her door open to get out.

"Hold up, hold up," Danez said.

"What?" Ronnisha asked. "What is it, Danez?" She couldn't help but see the serious look on Danez's face.

"I don't know if this Rain chick is gon' be up here today or not," Danez said. "But you know how me, Marquis, and Nieko feel about this chick. Somethin' just ain't right, but we don't know for sure."

"Okay," Ronnisha said, trying to figure out where Danez was going with what he was saying. "So, what do you want me to do? You know I'm here for you and Lamarcus and wanna help. Not wanna help. I am gonna help. Tell me, Danez."

"If you can," Danez said, clenching Ronnisha's thigh. "And I mean only if you get a little alone time, I want you to get a feel for this Rain chick. Don't say nothin' that is gonna tip her off or nothin' like that, but I just wanna know how you feel about her from talkin' to her. 'Cause, I swear, somethin' just don't seem right about this chick. But, then again, I know that sometimes I can overreact and stuff, so maybe I'm just trippin'. You the people person out of the two of us, so I know you'll get a good feel for the chick and let me know what you think."

"I will," Ronnisha said, leaning over and kissing Danez. "If she here, I'll see what she say and how she act and let you know."

Dressed in black, knee-high suede boots, tight white jeans, and a cut white, frilly shirt, Ronnisha walked behind Danez and into the hospital. The couple headed up the elevator, looking at one another. They both felt anxious. Ronnisha felt anxious because she was nervous, as the situation was so grave. Danez, on the other hand, was anxious because he wanted to see his friend and get the first-hand story about what happened. He would have gotten it when finding Lamarcus at his house, but it was so hard to understand what he was saying.

When Ronnisha and Danez stepped off of the elevator, they were quickly greeted by Miss Amber. She'd been coming from the bathroom and was headed back to her son's room. She smiled and turned, coming straight to Ronnisha. The two women greeted one another as they hugged. "Girl, you look cute today," Amber said.

Ronnisha thanked Miss Amber as she hugged Danez then stepped back. "How are you feeling?" Ronnisha asked. "I mean, I know you must be scared, but at least happy that Lamarcus is up and talking."

"Yeah," Amber said, nodding her head. "You could say that. The doctors, and I don't know if Danez told you, but the doctors said that he'd have to have a few operations because some of his nerves were damaged, and they're not sure if all of the surgeries will be successful, but I'm just happy that my son is alive and stuff. That's all I can really thank God for. I cannot lie, though. It is a little hard to understand him, at first. But, after he gets going and gets to talking quite a bit, it gets easier to understand him. His lips are still badly swollen, and I think a couple of his teeth were knocked out, but I can't be sure. I was just focused on talking to him."

"Okay, Miss Amber," Danez said. He wanted her to sit down so she wouldn't get too emotional talking about her son. "Do you mind if we go in there and talk to him or do you think that would be too much for him right now?"

Amber shrugged. "I mean," she said, looking down the bright, white hallway. "I think he would like that. He actually asked about you when I first went in and talked to him about an hour ago or so. I told him that you were up here and that you'd be back up. But, let me stop talkin', Baby. Go on in there and talk to him and stuff. The doctor said he got a little while before they do some sort of test or somethin' and that he wouldn't be available to talk to us. So, go on."

With Ronnisha at his side, Danez headed down the hallway. "You sure you want me to come in there with you?" Ronnisha asked. "I mean, do you think he would want me to see him lookin' like whatever he look like?"

"Ronnisha, Baby," Danez said. "He ain't like that, trust me. Just come in here and be you. I'm sure he'll be okay with it."

They walked up to the room and stepped inside. Hearing someone enter the room, Lamarcus turned and looked toward the doorway. He smiled when his eyes landed on Danez and Ronnisha.

"Fuck," Lamarcus said, smiling. "Here this nigga go."

Ronnisha giggled at Lamarcus and the humor in his voice, even in the worst of times. She walked over to his bruised, broken body and leaned in to gently hug him. "How are you feeling?" she asked, looking him up and down but trying not to stare.

Lamarcus chuckled – a chuckle that sounded forced, but genuine. "Well," he said, "I'm pretty fucked up. So, they doped me up pretty good. Too bad weed ain't legal in Indiana, or else I know they'd be givin' me some of that good medicinal shit when I get out."

Danez chuckled, noticing how Lamarcus' speech was a deep mumble. He looked back to make sure that no doctors were walking up on them. "Don't you worry about all that," Danez said, looking down at his best friend. "I'mma get with that one nigga we know and see about getting' you some of that good Colombian shit, okay? Don't you worry about that kinda shit. Whenever you get outta here, I'mma make sure that you feelin' real good when you do finally get outta here, okay?"

Lamarcus tried to nod, but his body was too numb to successfully do so. "Okay," he said.

Ronnisha stepped back to give Danez space. She made eye contact with Danez, asking him subliminally if it would be okay for her to stay. Danez pointed at the floor, letting Ronnisha know that her presence was welcomed and that she didn't need to go anywhere. With his hand gripping the metal bedrail, Danez looked into Lamarcus' eyes. "Tell me what happened, nigga," he said. "I need to hear from you what the fuck happened. You was try'na tell me some shit when I was bringin' you up here and shit, but I couldn't really understand you."

"Yeah," Lamarcus said. "I was pretty fucked up. Well, I still am." He looked away then back toward Danez. "It was that nigga Qoree, who think he run The Land. You know?"

"Yeah, you know we know the nigga," Danez said. "And you know the niggas in that hood say that nigga ain't shit, so he don't really run nothin'. But, anyway, go ahead."

"Me and Rain was at home, chillin', you know," Lamarcus explained, "and I coulda swore that I heard somethin'. So…So…" He lost his words for a moment as he tried to move his arm because it itched. "So, I got up and went over to the window and shit to look, you know. So, I look out and I don't see nothin', or at least I didn't think that I saw nothin'. When me and Rain went back to chillin' over on the couch, we both heard something. Like, this time, there was no doubt about it. By the time I was about to reach under the couch and get my gun and shit, next thing we know bullets is flyin' in the house. I swear, it was some shit like you see on the movies and shit in Los Angeles or somethin'. I don't know how many bullets that nigga pumped into my grandma house. It was so fucked up. I hurried up and got Rain down onto the floor and shit, by the couch, and waited. She was screamin' and shit, I felt so scared for her. I was just try'na make sure that nothin' bad happened to her, that's all."

Danez looked into Ronnisha's eyes for a few moments too long before looking back at Lamarcus. "So, what happened next?" he asked.

"Qoree and these three other niggas I never even seen before," Lamarcus said, "bust in the damn door and came into the living room. They knocked Rain out and took her into the other room, I guess. I don't really know where they took her. Then, Qoree held a gun to my head and made me go downstairs to the safe. Man, he took all the money outta there. I don't know what the fuck I'mma do, but the nigga made me open the safe and he took all the fuckin' money I had. I was just thinkin' like last week or sometime like that that I should spread that money out and not have it all in one fuckin' place, but I ain't think too much about it. Then this happened. Fuck."

"Don't start blamin' yourself," Danez said. "This is that nigga Qoree's fault and you know it. And don't worry about the money. You know we gon' get that shit back, and get that nigga Qoree."

"Yeah, well," Lamarcus said. "Then, we came back upstairs and I thought he was about to leave. The nigga talked a buncha shit about me and you bein' in his territory and all that kinda shit. He talked like he the king of that hood or somethin' when, like you said, them niggas over there don't even trust the nigga and don't even want him around. Then, the three niggas he had with him jumped on

92

me and just started kickin' and punchin' and shit like that, as you can see."

Ronnisha looked up and down Lamarcus' body, wondering just how many bones were broken. Parts of his body were covered with cast-like wrappings. She couldn't even begin to count the number of I.V. lines that were hooked into his body, let alone process the machines that stood at the back of his bed. She then thought about how she had meant to stop and get a flower or card for Lamarcus' mother, prompting her to make a mental note to get back to doing that.

"Next thing I know," Lamarcus said, "them niggas was liftin' me up and puttin' me up on the pool table. That's when shit got real fucked up. Qoree was slammin' a pool stick into my back and shit. Man, that shit hurt so bad. When he left, I managed to get off the pool table. I ain't think I was gon' make it, but I managed to use my arms and what little strength I had to get my ass over to the couch and find my phone. And that's when I called you."

Danez nodded, feeling anger build inside of him. Ronnisha, very tuned in with her man's feelings, rubbed Danez's shoulders. He glanced back at his woman – his queen – before putting his hand up on top of her hand.

"That's what I figured," Danez said. "I don't know if you mama told you and shit, but Marquis and Nieko was up here last night and shit."

"Yeah, she told me," Lamarcus said. "I know them niggas at work, but I'mma have to thank them for keepin' my mama company and stuff."

"Yeah, well," Danez said, "we rolled up to your house last night and went inside. A cop came up here. That doctor, the black one, said she had to call as a part of hospital policy or somethin'. I ain't tell him shit other than that I found you and shit, 'cause you know how I feel about cops."

"Coo," Lamarcus said. "So what you find at the house?"

Danez shrugged his shoulders. "Just what you said," he responded. "Look like the place got shot up somethin' fucked up. We went down in the basement and saw that the safe was empty. Then we looked around, thinking that you mighta spread your money out – hopin' that you did some shit like that – , but, like you said, you ain't do that. It look like he got you for every fuckin' dollar you had in that safe."

Lamarcus looked ahead, feeling so much regret. He couldn't help but doubt himself and wonder where he'd gone wrong. "I shoulda seen that shit comin'," he said. "I mean, back when I was stayin' over in the hood and shit, I would know when a fuckin' squirrel was comin' up to the house to climb a tree. I shoulda known them niggas was out in the yard. That just go to show that you can't let your guard down for one second when it come to these niggas nowadays. I don't know why I ain't have my gun ready. But you know what I thought about when I first woke up? I thought about how the fuck Qoree would even know where I live. I mean, I know I be havin' get-togethers and stuff, but I only have coo people over to my house – people that wouldn't even be havin' my name in they mouth, and especially not to no nigga like Qoree."

Once again, Danez looked at Ronnisha. She stepped away, to give her man and his boy even more space. "Yeah, I don't know," Danez said. "It was probably somebody that you know, but then again, I don't know. For all we know, that nigga Qoree could know some chick that work at the light company or the water company or somewhere like that."

"Yeah," Lamarcus said, looking away. "I don't know, but I keep thinkin' about that shit."

No sooner than Lamarcus uttered those words, the sound of heels slamming against the hospital tile echoed down the hall. Within seconds, Rain came walking into the hospital room. She smiled and waved at Lamarcus, rushing over to lean down and kiss him. "Oh my God, you're up," she said. "You're up."

Danez, looking Rain up and down, stepped back and stood next to Ronnisha. Yet again, they made prolonged eye contact. Ronnisha, feeling ready to find out what kind of vibe Rain gave off, introduced herself. Rain, smiling as if she were a businesswoman putting on her best face, hugged Ronnisha and told her it was nice to meet her before turning back around to Lamarcus.

"Are you okay, Baby?" Lamarcus asked, looking into Rain's eyes with caring eyes. "All I could think about was how I didn't want you to get hurt."

"I'm okay," Rain said, pointing at her head where there was a bump. "I mean, they hit me pretty hard, but that's all. Thanks to your friend Danez here, you was able to get to the hospital quick and stuff, so that's good. Are you feeling any pain? What's happening next? When do you think you'll be getting out of here?"

Danez stepped in front of Rain briefly. "Excuse me," he said. "Hey, Lamarcus, we gon' step out in the hallway real quick, okay, so you can talk to your lady."

"Oh, thank you so much," Rain said, looking at Danez. "Are you gonna be headed home soon, Danez?"

Danez hesitated to answer. He found the question to be odd, especially in these circumstances and because they really didn't know each other that well. However, he knew he needed to remain cordial, not only for his boy Lamarcus, but also in case he turned out to be wrong about Rain. "I don't know yet," he answered. "Maybe." He hesitated, looking for his words. "Just go on and talk to Lamarcus. We gon' step out into the hallway."

Ronnisha smiled at Rain then Lamarcus before following Danez out into the hallway. Once they were several feet away from the hospital room doorway, Danez pulled her to the side.

"Yeah," Ronnisha said, looking back toward the room. "Somethin' is up with her."

"What you mean?" Danez asked. "I mean, I know what you mean, but I wanna know what you really mean."

"I mean," Ronnisha said. "I mean, she was almost too happy."

"Too happy?" Danez asked.

"Yeah," Ronnisha asked. "Did you see the way she came in that room with that forced smile. Think about it. It's almost like she is try'na force herself to not come across guilty or somethin', I don't know. Everything about her just seem fake. But I gotta talk to her a little bit before I can really know, I guess. I just saw the chick for a split second."

Ronnisha and Danez went back out into the waiting area and sat next to Amber. Amber then jumped up, saying that she was going to go and grab something to eat. "Can you tell Lamarcus before you leave, please, that I'm goin' downstairs to get somethin' to eat?"

"Of course," Ronnisha answered, patting Amber's arm. "We will."

Amber disappeared, getting onto an elevator. Ronnisha looked at Danez, who was grinding his teeth. "Don't," she said. "Just don't think that deep about it yet."

"I can't help it," Danez said, standing up. "That nigga Qoree coulda killed Lamarcus. You saw him, Ronnisha. Didn't you? You saw him?"

Ronnisha was at a loss for words, as she knew just what Danez meant. She wasn't sure she'd ever seen anyone as beat up as Lamarcus. It almost seemed unreal; it almost seemed like something out of a movie. She watched as Danez paced around in the waiting area, drawing the attention of other people sitting around. She stood up and grabbed Danez's wrist. "Calm down," she said. "Baby, calm down."

"I'm tryin'," Danez said. He then pointed at Lamarcus' hospital room. "Somethin' tells me that chick in there that he lookin' at with them googly eyes and shit had somethin' to do with this shit. Somethin' about her just don't sit well with me. Shit, I wouldn't be surprised if she set him up so she could get the money and now she gon' be smilin' in his face like ain't nothin' happen and she ain't have nothin' to do with it."

Just as Ronnisha was about to speak, she noticed a doctor – tall, thin black woman – heading into Lamarcus' room. She pointed and directed Danez's attention to the hallway. The two of them watched as the doctor went in and Rain came walking out, heading toward the waiting area.

"I'mma go outside or downstairs for a second, okay?" Danez said. "Talk to oh girl and see what you feel about her and what she say, okay?"

Ronnisha nodded. "Okay," she said. "I will."

Danez headed over to the elevator, nodding at Rain. "You're not headed home are you, Danez?" Rain asked.

"Naw," Danez said, brushing past her. "Just goin' to get somethin' to eat and some air."

"Oh, okay," Rain said. She then turned toward Ronnisha, smiling. She came over and sat down next to her. Ronnisha watched as she pulled tissue out of her Tory Burch handbag and wiped her puffy eyes. "Oh, this is so sad."

"Yeah," Ronnisha said, glancing over at Rain. "It is. It really is." She thought about how she needed to say something that would really get Rain talking. This would be the only way to pick up on what kind of chick she was, and if she had anything to do with what happened to Lamarcus. "All I could really think about was you, girl, when I heard about what happened."

"Me?" Rain asked, looking at Ronnisha and smiling. "Really, girl. That is so nice."

"Yeah," Ronnisha said. "I just think about what another woman goes through. I imagine it must have been a really terrifying situation for you. I just thank God that I've never been in your shoes."

"Yeah," Rain said, looking away and down at the floor. "It truly was horrible."

"I mean, what all happened?" Ronnisha asked. "I heard secondhand from Danez, but I didn't know exactly what happened."

"Well," Rain said. "Me and Lamarcus were kicking it and stuff, you know." She crossed her legs. "And we thought we heard something outside. At first, we shook it off. Then, we heard it again. And that's when it all began. Bullets started flying into the house and stuff. Glass was busting everywhere. I thought I was going to die."

Ronnisha shook her head. "I bet you did," she said. "I mean, that sounds really horrible."

"Yeah," Rain said. "We were on the ground. I musta been screaming like a horror movie or something. Then, when the bullets finally stopped, that's when Qoree and his boys came through the door. Just when stuff got quiet, we looked up and saw them. It was so terrifying. The house was dark, shot up, then we look up and see three niggas standin' in the doorway. We hadn't even heard the door being kicked in because there were so many bullets flying."

"Damn, girl," Ronnisha said, rubbing Rain's forearm. "That sounds really horrible."

"Yeah," Rain said. "But, you know, I was so terrified that I was just beggin' for my life… Beggin' to not be killed and stuff. Then, next thing you know, I wake up on the couch in the front room. They knocked me out, so I didn't know what they were doing with Lamarcus and stuff. Next thing I know Danez is there, looking into my face and stuff. He took us to the hospital. I swear I thought Lamarcus was going to die when we was on our way up here, but, by the grace of God, that didn't happen. Thank you, Lord." Rain pressed the palms of her hands together and closed her eyes briefly.

Ronnisha turned away from Rain and rolled her eyes. Something about this chick Rain was just so fake. Ronnisha almost wanted to throw up. However, she knew she needed to keep going, or at least use the time that Danez and Amber were away wisely. "You ever seen Qoree and his dudes before?"

Rain looked at Ronnisha. "Have I ever seen them before?" she asked, not realizing that she was repeating the question. "I mean, no. No, I haven't. Last night... Last night was the first time I'd ever seen them niggas. And I hope I don't ever have to see them again. That shit was too scary."

"But why?" Ronnisha asked. "I mean, why would they do somethin' like this to Lamarcus?" Ronnisha noticed how Rain was not making constant eye contact.

"I don't know," Rain said, shaking her head. "That's the same thing I was try'na think about last night. It was so hard to go asleep because all I could think about was how Lamarcus could have been killed and stuff. When I first saw his body in the hospital room right there, I wanted to break down in tears. I've never seen anything like that."

"Yeah," Ronnisha said, shaking her head. "It's pretty bad. I was thinkin' the same damn thing, girl. But that's what we try'na figure out."

"We?" Rain asked. "What you mean? And try'na figure out what?"

"You know Lamarcus and Danez are like this," Ronnisha said, twisting her index fingers around one another. "They like brothers, if not even closer than that. And Danez is mad as fuck."

"Yeah," Rain said, looking at the floor. "I bet he is. I would be too. It's gonna be hard to move on from this."

"Oh, no," Ronnisha said. "That's not gon' happen, I can tell you that."

"What's not gon' happen?" Rain asked, sounding concerned.

"Ain't nobody gon' be letting this go, trust me," Ronnisha said. "Danez is already determined to not only find Qoree and his boys that helped do this fucked up shit, but he also is lookin' for the nigga who set this shit up. Shit, Danez is probably even madder at that person for helping."

"Oh, no," Rain said. "I mean, I don't like violence. I don't know if that's the way to go."

Ronnisha shrugged. "Well, somebody is gon' have to pay," she said. "I just wonder who it gon' be. Whoever they is, it's gon' be bad."

Rain could feel her heart thumping in her chest. She was happy the human body had been made to operate silently. Otherwise, the entire hospital could very well be shaking like an earthquake from how hard her heart was thumping. She couldn't look Ronnisha in the eye.

"So," Rain said, ready to change the conversation as Qoree's words were on her mind. "How long have you and Danez been together?"

Ronnisha looked at Rain, wondering why she would be asking such a question. "A good minute," she answered. "That's my bae, you know." She smiled.

"That's nice," Rain said. "Y'all moved in together yet and stuff?"

Ronnisha nodded. "I mean, yeah," she answered. "Been livin' together for a minute now."

"That's nice," Rain said, thinking.

Just then, Danez got off the elevator and came walking over toward Ronnisha and Rain. Ronnisha stood up as Danez approached.

"Hey, Baby," Danez said. "I just got a call about some business, so we gon' have to roll out for a little bit. We can come up here later on."

Rain stood up. "You guys headed home, then?" she asked, rather anxiously.

Ronnisha and Danez locked eyes before Danez turned toward Rain and answered, "Yeah, something like that."

"Yeah, well, I'm about to head out myself so I can get my day going," Rain said. "I hate to leave Lamarcus up here, but I gotta help my family with something. I'll probably be back up here tonight myself, but I'm not sure what time."

The three of them walked to Lamarcus' room to say goodbye to him. The elevator ride down to the parking garage was long and rather quiet, as Danez and Ronnisha stood on one side with Rain on the other. Danez wanted so badly to grab Rain by her shoulders and shake the truth out of her, but he knew that if he did such a thing in view of the security camera, there would probably be security guards waiting for him on the ground floor.

"Well, it was nice meeting you," Rain said to Ronnisha, hugging her softly. "I'll see you two up here later on, I guess."

"Yeah, girl," Ronnisha said. "It was nice meeting you, too."

Ronnisha walked hand and hand with Danez over to Danez's SUV and got inside while Rain walked over to her car and did the same. She waited on Danez and Ronnisha to pull out before she did. The two cars, back to back, exited the parking garage and were now out on the streets of the east side. Rain allowed some space to build between her car and Danez's SUV as she followed them toward downtown.

"That chick," Ronnisha said, looking over to Danez. "Somethin' don't seem right about her."

"Exactly," Danez said. "I don't trust her one fuckin' bit. I saw Amber downstairs and you know how she is. She was talkin' about how bad she wanted to jump on Rain when she saw her up there. And I think she was really gon do it if she had the chance. What did she say to you?"

Ronnisha quickly went over the conversation with Rain. She and Danez both concluded that it was very strange for Rain to ask if they lived together, and for her to be so preoccupied with whether or not they were headed home.

Ronnisha, being as observant as ever, noticed that the same kind of car that Rain had walked toward was following behind them a couple of blocks. "Danez," she said, pointing at the rearview mirror. "Look. The green car like a block or two back."

Danez looked in his rearview mirror then to Ronnisha. "Yeah," he said. "What about it?"

"Is that Rain?" she asked. "I think it is, Danez. She was walkin' toward a car that look just like that."

"Oh, yeah?" Danez said. He then switched lanes and quickly got into a turn lane to turn left and head south. "Let's see if it's her and if she followin' us."

Danez turned onto Sherman Avenue and headed south. He and Ronnisha watched the rearview mirror closely. Next thing they knew, the green car was turning as well.

"She followin' us," Ronnisha said. "I swear, I really think she is. That bitch is followin' us."

100

"That's why she wanted to know where we live so bad," Danez said. "She got somethin' invested in this shit. I know she do."

Danez and Ronnisha knew they needed to lose this chick Rain so she wouldn't know where they lived downtown. Danez turned a few corners and made his way north to Tenth Street. There, he pulled into a busy Kroger parking lot. He parked in a spot that faced the street. Within seconds, they watched as the green car rolled down Tenth Street, doing the same big circle that they'd just done. And they could see into the window that Rain was behind the wheel. Danez turned his head and looked at Ronnisha. Ronnisha looked away, shaking her head. "Her," she said.

"Yup," Danez said, nodding his head. "I knew somethin' was up with her. And now we know what."

CHAPTER 10

Danez rolled over to his convenience store on Clifton, which was on the west side of The Land. Ronnisha waited out in the SUV while Danez went inside to talk to a couple of his employees, as well as count some of the money. While she sat there all she could think about was how a perfectly fine moment could turn ugly in a matter of seconds. She truly wondered if this Qoree guy knew about Danez's businesses. And if he did, how long would it be before he came up to one of them looking for Danez?

Ronnisha was happy to see Danez coming back out to the SUV. He climbed in and pulled out of the parking lot. Danez could pick up on the fact that Ronnisha was a bit worried. "You okay over there, Baby?" he asked.

"I mean, yeah," Ronnisha said, shrugging. "Just over here thinking about what that Qoree dude might know about your businesses and stuff. You don't think he'll ever come up here and try to get you up here, do you?"

"I wish a nigga would," Danez said, shaking his head. "There would be a full-blown shoot-out between me and that nigga. You know me, I don't go down easy."

"Yeah, but I just think we need to get ahead of it before it gets ahead of us even more," Ronnisha said. "I mean, you saw how just a minute ago that Rain chick was try'na follow us."

"I know," Danez said. "That's why I got my queen by my side. If it wasn't for you, we wouldn't even have seen that shit."

Just then, Ronnisha thought of the perfect way she could get out and about and talk to people to see what she could find out. "You know what?" she said. "I got an idea."

Quickly, Danez turned the radio down. "What?"

"There is this salon that me and Tyne used to go to over here, on Thirtieth Street," Ronnisha said. "And you can just about find out anything about any nigga up in there."

"So, what you sayin'?" Danez asked. "You not sayin' that you go up in there and just start askin' questions about this shit, are you? Naw, Baby." He shook his head. "I can't let your name and face get twisted up in this shit even more than it might be already. I already feel a little bad for havin' you sit there and talk to that Rain chick, 'cause now we know that she ain't real. Now we know that she up to somethin'. For all we know, she runnin' back to Qoree and tellin' him what the fuck you was sayin' and stuff."

"Yeah, but I ain't tell her nothin' that people can't already know," Ronnisha said. "And, no. I'm sayin' I can go up in there and get my hair done and shit and just talk and see what they can tell me. I bet them women in that salon know somethin' about this Qoree dude. If he got money and is well known, they'll know about him and will spill it just to be talkin' and stuff."

Danez spent the next few minutes contemplating Ronnisha's idea. "You think you can handle it?" he asked, with skepticism.

Ronnisha picked her purse up off of the floor from between her feet and reached in. "I guess you forget who I am," she said. "You know I got this, Baby. When we get back to the apartment, I'mma call Tyne and get the number to that salon and see if I can squeeze in there today or somethin' to get a little something." She pulled the mirror above her seat down and looked into it. "Plus," she said, "I could use my edges touched up. I'm startin' to look a little raggedy around there."

Danez chuckled. "Yeah," he said, "I was thinkin' the same thing. Lookin' like little bushes."

Ronnisha looked back over at Danez and pushed her hand into her purse again. "Nigga, you better stop," she said, smiling, "before I get you before Qoree do."

Danez chuckled.

When they got back to their apartment, Ronnisha quickly got on the phone as Danez made some calls in the bedroom about some connects he had that were coming up in trucks from Louisville. She called Tyne, hoping that she wasn't at work yet.

"Hello?" Tyne answered, sounding snappy.

"Well, hello to you too," Ronnisha said. "Girl, what is goin' on with you."

"Girl, nothin'," Tyne answered. "Not a damn thing. Just saw that chick again."

"Girl, don't get into another fight with her," Ronnisha warned. "It ain't even worth your time."

"Oh, I know," Tyne said. "She looked down at the ground and kept goin'. I looked at her like yeah, that's right, bitch. Walk on by, walk on by, walk on by."

Ronnisha shook her head, always finding it funny when Tyne would quote old school songs. "Girl, anyway, what are you doin'?" she asked.

"On my way into this fuckin' job right now," she answered. "Thinkin' about how I hope this manager I got that be breathin' down my neck ain't there. Wassup, though? You go up to the hospital with Danez and see Lamarcus yet or what?"

"Yeah," Ronnisha answered. "He pretty messed up. It was almost unbearable to see, girl. I mean, really. He look like he could have died. All types of machines hooked up to his body and stuff."

"That sound horrible as fuck," Tyne said.

"But, girl, that's not why I'm callin' you," Ronnisha said. "Remember that hair salon we used to go to over on Thirtieth Street where them chicks be spillin' it all up in there?"

"Girl, yes," Tyne answered. "Urban Beauty is what it's called. I don't go there no more because they just talk too much about anyone and everyone up in there. I just couldn't take it no more."

"Girl, I need the number to that lady in there, if you still got it," Ronnisha said. "I need to slide on up in there real quick to get these edges redone."

"Yeah, you do," Tyne said. "I was thinkin' the same thing, but I ain't wanna say nothin'. 'Cause you know how you get."

Ronnisha rolled her eyes. "Damn, what is this today?" she asked rhetorically. "Is this shit on Ronnisha's hair today or something or what?"

"Girl, calm down," Tyne said. "You be doin' the most. Yeah, I still got the number in my phone. I can get off here and text it to you when I pull up at this stoplight comin' up."

"Okay," Ronnisha said. "Girl, do that ASAP so I can slide on in there."

"Okay," Tyne said. "And when I get off work later on, girl, I wanna talk and stuff, okay?"

"Okay, girl," Ronnisha said. "Just go on and text me the number to that one lady so I can hit her up, okay?"

Tyne and Ronnisha ended the phone call just as Danez was walking back into the living room. He grabbed his jacket and keys, clearly headed out the door. "You get the chick's number or what?"

"Yeah," Ronnisha answered. Just then, her phone vibrated. "Tyne just sent it to me and I'mma see if I can slide up in there today or somethin'."

"And you sure you got this?" Danez asked.

"Nigga, yes," Ronnisha said. "I'mma just go up in there and drop a couple hints or somethin', somethin' like I met this nigga name Qoree or somethin' and see what them hens up in there start sayin'. I know they'll know somethin'. They know every nigga in this whole damn city. They the kinda chicks that be at every party, at every concert, Black Expo, and everything. Shit, I wouldn't be surprised if they knew just where the nigga live and stuff, but we'll see. If he get around at all, then they'll know somethin' about him and shit."

"Okay, Baby," Danez said. He walked over to Ronnisha as she stood up. He slapped her ass then they kissed. "Just remember what I said. Be careful and shit and watch your fuckin' back 'cause you don't know who doin' what out here. And make sure you don't say nothin' to them chicks in that salon about me in case they cool with Qoree or somethin'."

"I won't," Ronnisha said, "and okay, go on and do what you gotta do."

"Yeah, gotta go meet these niggas comin' up from down south," Danez said. "Let me know how it go, okay?"

Danez left as Ronnisha called the number Tyne sent to her in the text message.

"Hello?" a woman answered with the sound of women talking in the background. "This is Sharon."

"Miss Sharon?" Ronnisha asked. "This is Ronnisha. I don't know if you remember me, but I used to come in there with my girl Tyne."

"Girl, yes I do," Sharon said, sounding pleased. "Girl, how have you been? And, of course, I remember you. You had that good thick hair. How have you been, Ronnisha?"

"Girl, I'm doin' okay," Ronnisha asked. "That's actually why I'm callin' you. I need to see about slidin' in and doin' something with this head. It ain't too bad, but I know I need to do somethin' about these edges. You think you can help me out today or sometime real soon or somethin'?"

"Hell yeah," Sharon said. "Actually, Ronnisha, if you wanna come up in here around three o'clock, that would work great. I had this one woman cancel on me this morning, so you more than welcome to have her spot if you want. Would that work for you?"

Ronnisha pulled her phone away from her face and looked at the time. "Yeah," she said. "I can be up in there around three. Thank you so much."

"Yeah, it might be kinda crazy up in here around then, but I'll get you together real nice," Sharon said. "Don't you worry."

"Okay, Miss Sharon," Ronnisha said, smiling. "See you in a little bit."
***

Miss Sharon welcomed Ronnisha into the shop with a big smile and her arms wide open. When Ronnisha walked into the salon, she immediately noticed the number of women around. There was no doubt that the stylists were making money. And this was especially so because a few major Indianapolis events were coming up to usher the city into the holiday season. Numerous hood chicks sat around in chairs getting their hair done, everything from 27-pieces to micro braids to twisties to finger waves.

Being her usual, nice self, Ronnisha waved at everyone and spoke as she made her way over to Sharon. Sharon, who was quickly approaching 40 years old but tried to look every bit of 25, wrapped her arms around Ronnisha and smiled. Ronnisha immediately noticed how nothing about the woman had changed. She still had bright red hair, long fingernails, and a couple of gold teeth in the front that shined in the light.

"Girl, sit down, Ronnisha," Sharon insisted. "Girl, please, sit down."

Ronnisha sat down in the chair then turned around to face the mirror. "Miss Sharon," she said, smiling and nodding as she looked at how she'd upgraded her booth. "How have you been lately? I swear, I been thinkin' about you a lot."

"Well, you musta not been thinkin' about me all that much," Sharon said, her Georgia accent coming out when she spoke. "'Cause if you was, you woulda came up in here with these edges. Girl, what have you been doin'? You been out jogging and stuff with the white people and sweating or somethin'?"

Ronnisha snickered and shook her head. "Miss Sharon," she said. "Yeah, I guess you could say somethin' like that. I just been busy."

"Hmm, hmm," Sharon said, squinting at Ronnisha in the mirror. "I know how it is to be young. I'm still there. I stay busy myself."

"Miss Sharon," Ronnisha said, "why don't you stop?"

"Can't stop, won't stop," Sharon said. "I'm too young to stop."

"When you gon' slow down and have you some kids, Miss Sharon?" Ronnisha asked. "I mean, girl, think about it. I feel like you would be a great mother. For real, girl. You should have you some kids."

As Sharon stepped up to the counter to grab some supplies, she shook her head quickly. "Awe naw," she said. "I'm too young for all that." She then ran her hand over her stomach. "I already know what's gon' happen if I have some kids. I'mma get all fat and then I ain't gon' be able to pull these young niggas like I do when I walk down the street."

Ronnisha, not realizing that she was doing so, rolled her eyes. "Okay," she said, "if you say so, Miss Sharon."

"Roll your eyes again, girl," Sharon said, smiling. "And you gon' find out what it's like to walk out the hair salon with a bald head and stuff."

"You wouldn't do that, would you, Miss Sharon?" Ronnisha asked.

Sharon raised her eyebrows. She then turned around and asked Ronnisha what she wanted to do with her hair. Knowing that her purse was stacked with money, Ronnisha didn't particularly care. "Girl, do what you want," she said. "Just make my hair look good and simple, so I ain't lookin' all ghetto and stuff."

"So what you try'na say about my red hair?" Sharon asked. She then tapped Ronnisha's shoulder. "Girl, I'm just playin'. Okay," she paused to take a good look at Ronnisha's head, "I know what I can do."

Sharon went on with starting on Ronnisha's head. "So, girl," she said, "what have you been up to? You still with that nigga? What's his name?"

"You talkin' about Danez," Ronnisha said. "And yeah, I am. You know that's my boo."

"Hmm, hmm," Sharon said, her voice full of skepticism. "I remember when I had boos and baes and boo thangs. I still do, but I just ain't got time to deal with them like that. Plus, these niggas nowadays don't even be try'na spend money on a bitch like they should. And girl, you know I can't stand no broke man. If a man ain't got no money, don't talk to me. I just ain't got time for that."

"I feel you on that," Ronnisha said. "Yeah, me and Danez been doin' real good. I actually just left the apartment and he was there. "

"Hmm, hmm," Sharon said. "Girl, I forget. Where y'all stay now?"

Ronnisha knew she had better not let anyone know, especially in the hood, where she and Danez lived. Therefore, she lied and said, "Over on the east side. Not too far from the mall."

"I see, I see," Sharon said. "You not one of these chicks out here talkin' about havin' his baby and stuff, is you?"

"Girl, no," Ronnisha said, shaking her head. "I'm too young to be doin' all that. I still got too much to do with my life."

"Oh, so you workin' now?" Sharon asked.

Ronnisha giggled. "Nope," she said. "I mean, I keep my eye open for jobs and stuff that I might like, but, no, I ain't workin'. I know I need to be."

"I mean, if you got a man that got it, then what's the problem?" Sharon asked. "Girl, if I was you, I'd be savin' whatever money he gave me so that whenever he act up, you will be okay and stuff to be on your own. I'm tellin' you, girl, in my thirty years," she smirked, knowing she'd just told a lie about her age, "I ain't never took no shit off no man. Say the wrong thing to me and I will be gone before you get home from doin' whatever the fuck you doin'."

"Naw, Miss Sharon," Ronnisha said. "Everything really is okay." Ronnisha then went over a few thoughts that had crossed her mind on her way over to the shop. "But right now he try'na catch up with an old friend of his."

A darker-skinned chick had just finished getting a relaxer in the chair next to Ronnisha. When Sharon turned the chair a little bit, Ronnisha and the chick made eye contact. Ronnisha nodded and asked how she was, getting a bit of a smile in response. She then focused her attention back to Sharon. "He try'na do this thing where they have a get-together and stuff," she said. "So far, he done got in touch with a few dudes that he used to hang with, and it's gonna be real nice to catch up with all of them after all this time. But he still got a couple that he just can't seem to find online or nothin', and he kinda down about it. So, I'm try'na help him find them, or at least this one. You know how it is when you playin' wifey."

"Who, girl?" Sharon asked. "You know I be out at the club every Thursday, Friday, and Saturday night. And shit, girl, I done even found some motorcycle clubs that I hang out around. You know I love a room full of men, especially when they get to drinking." She laughed out loud. "Girl, I be talkin' them niggas out of their wallet. And they be handin' them right on over like they payin' child support or alimony to a bitch. Yes, honey!"

"Dang, Miss Sharon," Ronnisha said, hoping that Sharon would know the name she was about to drop. "You ain't gotta be like that. But anyway, I know you probably don't know some of the other ones 'cause they moved down to Louisville a long time ago."

"Awe, naw," Sharon said. "I mean, I used to go down to Louisville for Derby and stuff, but that's it. Outside of that, I don't really know nothin' else about that place except that it sit on the Ohio River. And even then, I ain't too sure if I'm fade, so there you go."

"I feel you, Miss Sharon," Ronnisha said. "But, no, the dude we havin' the hardest time catchin' up to is this dude named Qoree."

"Qoree?" Sharon asked. She stopped working on Ronnisha's hair to think for a moment. "Wait a minute," she said. "I feel like I might know him. You wouldn't happen to know what he look like, would you?"

Ronnisha lightly shrugged. "Yes and no," she said. "But not really. I know I used to see him somewhere over in The Land a long time ago, but I really didn't know him like that."

"Over in The Land?" Sharon asked, looking into Ronnisha's eyes in the mirror. She then nodded her head emphatically. "Yup, I know that nigga," she said. "I was at this club, and I don't remember which one, so don't ask. But, anyway, I was at this club and this younger dude was pushin' up on me like he wanted some of this vintage vagina."

"Miss Sharon!" Ronnisha said, sounding outraged. "Girl, you ain't have to go there with me."

"I use vintage because I know I got that good shit," Sharon said. "But, anyway, like I was sayin'. He was pushin' up on me, but he real aggressive. Long story short, is started to see him around The Land 'cause I got some cousins who stay over there, where I used to stay on California, you know, and they used to hang out with that nigga. I didn't hang out with him but a couple times when he was over there smokin' with them and stuff. I didn't remember him at first until we got to talkin'. And then I knew who he was. I knew he had somethin' for me, but I was nice and turned him away. He used to stay down on…down on…" Sharon tried her hardest to pull her memories to the front of her mind. She'd been smoking the best quality of weed since the late nineties, so it wasn't unheard of for her to be forgetful. However, all she needed was a little time and, usually, things would come flooding back. "I know," she said, her eyes opening wide. "He lived down in his house on White. You know, that street that's like three blocks long and stuff, down by the park? He was stayin' in this house behind them factories off of Montcalm, but I don't know if he still over there. I can ask my cousins if they still kick it with him from time to time and let you know."

Ronnisha smiled. "Could you please, Miss Sharon?" she asked. "I would really appreciate it if you could because Danez been practically beatin' himself up to get in touch with that nigga and I said I would ask around when I come in here and stuff. They just wanna catch up."

"Yeah, of course," Sharon said, not feeling any suspicion. "I mean, I'm not gon' tell my cousins that I'm lookin' for his ass, 'cause he might be try'na get up in this wet-wet again and I ain't got time for all that. But I will see what my cousin's know. As a matter of fact, one of them is supposed to be at my place right now with this little bad-ass kid they got. I hope that little nigga ain't tearin' up my shit or else I'mma have to tear up that ass when I get there. And if they mama wanna get mad, then she and her mama and her damn grandma can get it too."

Ronnisha shook her hand. "I swear, Miss Sharon," she said, "you be doin' the most."

110

Ronnisha quickly changed the topic of the conversation. Unbeknownst to her, however, the dark-skinned chick in the chair next to her was listening with an open ear. Little did Ronnisha know, this female was closer to Qoree than she'd ever imagined. If Ronnisha had known such, she would never have opened her mouth to Miss Sharon.

Chapter 11

Chocolate Bunny, whose government name was Lala, sat in Qoree's house with a bitter taste in her mouth. If her hair had not just been done, she probably would have spent a good amount of energy breaking any and everything in sight. She was that mad about what she'd heard at the beauty shop – her man Qoree was pushing up on some old hag that was nowhere near as sexy as she was.

"Fuck that nigga," Lala groaned to herself. "How the fuck he gon' try to get with some chick that look like that bitch Sharon up at that shop? She ain't got no class or nothin' like that, especially not compared to me. I mean, that just don't make no sense."

Lala sat on Qoree's couch, having let herself in with the key he'd given her just a few weeks ago. For the first time in a long time, she thought that she'd finally found a dude that could be down for her. Her heart had been played with so much that at 21 years old, she'd basically given up on love. Then, Qoree came along and practically knocked her off of her feet. He took her shopping, spent however much money she wanted on whatever she wanted, and was just as much of a freak as she was. Now, she was second guessing it all as she sat on his couch and looked around. "I shoulda known," Lala said to herself. "I shoulda known that all this shit was too good to be true. Shit," she shrugged, "for all I know this nigga got a baby mama and a gang of kids somewhere. I still ain't met his family." She shook her head. "I'mma ask that nigga 'bout that."

When Lala had walked through the door on Thursday evening, she sent a text message to Qoree, asking him when he'd be home. He assured her that he would be on his way shortly and that they would be going out to eat at a nice seafood restaurant downtown. At first, Lala was going to send a nasty and thorough message to Qoree. She was going to let him know exactly how she was feeling right then. She then smiled, telling herself that it would be better to take the classy route. She was done with the ghetto drama after the last dude secretly had her on the side of his wife and children up in Lafayette, a small city a little less than halfway between Indianapolis and Chicago. On top of that, she wanted to see Qoree sweat a little bit. She wanted to see how he would explain what she'd heard without saying any names.

Twenty minutes or so passed with Lala drowning in her thoughts before Qoree pulled up out front, pulling partially up into the grass of the front yard. "Here this lyin' ass nigga come," Lala said.

Lala waited and seconds later, Qoree came walking through the front door. "Hey, wassup up, Chocolate?" Qoree asked, sounding very upbeat.

"Hi," Lala said in response.

Qoree shut the door and looked over at Lala. "You all right?" he asked, looking her up and down. "Your hair look on point."

"Thank you," Lala said, moving her neck to the side. "I'm glad you like it, since you like so much nowadays. And a lot of variety."

"What is up with you?" Qoree asked. Not waiting for a response, he carried some bags into the kitchen and lifted them up onto the counter.

Lala, hating to be ignored, quickly jumped up and headed over to the counter that separated the family room from the kitchen and dining area. "Is there somethin' you wanna tell me?"

Qoree looked at Lala. He always hated when a woman stepped out of line and caught an attitude with him. He'd been having a nice day, making money and enjoying the mild fall weather while it lasted. Qoree had even gone to get his car washed, just to add to his swagged out persona. "Wassup, Chocolate?" he asked, smiling and leaning over the counter. "Why are you coming at me with this attitude?"

Not being able to help herself, and hating when a man would lie to her face as if she couldn't tell, Lala reached out and slapped Qoree across the face. "Nigga, don't play stupid with me!" she yelled. "I know you been fuckin' around on me, or at least tryin' to."

Grabbing the side of his stinging face, Qoree quickly walked out of the kitchen. He now faced Lala, clearly very angry. "What the fuck was that for?" he asked. "And what the fuck is you talkin' about you crazy ass bitch?"

"What the fuck did you just call me?" Lala asked. Being called out of her name was something she never put up with, and especially not from a man. "You not gon' call me no bitch." Again, she slapped Qoree across the face.

Not being able to take anymore, Qoree grabbed Lala by her arms and gently pushed her back to the couch. "Calm the fuck down," he told her, now towering over her. "Calm the fuck down

113

and sit down. I told you I ain't been fuckin' around on you, so I don't even know where the fuck you would even get somethin' like that from."

"Oh, you don't," Lala said, standing up. She then pushed Qoree back a few feet from her and started to wave her arms about. "I was up at the hair salon today, as you know," she pointed at her hair, "and I heard about you nigga."

"Heard what?" Qoree said. "I don't even be out like that, so I don't even know what the fuck you could be talkin' about. I swear, I don't even know what the hell you sayin'."

"Sharon?" Lala asked, looking directly into Qoree's eyes. "You know what the fuck I'm talkin' about. Today, this chick came into the salon while I was gettin' my hair done and she was askin' Sharon if she know you because her nigga is try'na get in touch with you. Anyway, Sharon and her forty-year-old self did in fact know you. She even went as far as talkin' about how you was try'na push up on her at some club somewhere and get up in that old ass coochie she got that probably smell like some rotten ass, dead fish some fisherman pulled up outta the White River downtown. Don't play me, nigga. You know what the fuck I'm talkin' about. That old bitch stay with red hair…hair so damn red that that shit probably glow in the dark."

Qoree shook his head. "I know who you talkin' about," he said. "I hang with some of her cousins sometime. She think any nigga that say hello or hola to her want her, and I swear to God and put that on my child that I ain't never tried to push up on her. You talkin' about the chick with gold teeth?"

"Hmm, hmm," Lala said. "And how I'm supposed to know that you not lyin'? Huh? How?"

"'Cause, Baby," Qoree said. "That chick be full of herself and stuff. And why would I go gettin' some chick like that when I got my Chocolate Bunny right here. I swear, Baby. You are trippin' just like she be trippin'. Ain't nobody try to push up on her. She just one of them old bitches that think she still young and that young dudes want her because she squeeze herself into tight clothes and got red hair. I was prolly just talkin' to her, you know, in a friendly way and she took that and ran with it so she could have my name in her mouth."

114

Lala took a good, long moment to look at Qoree. "Nigga, you betta not be lyin' to me," she said. "I swear, if I hear that you messed around any, you gon' be sorry. I don't put up with that kinda shit anymore."

Qoree, talking very suavely, leaned in and tried to kiss Lala on the lips. She quickly turned her head to the side, causing Qoree to kiss her cheek gently. "Baby, why don't you just calm the fuck down?" Qoree asked. He then turned around and went and grabbed a bottle of red wine he'd stopped and gotten at a winery downtown on his way up from the south side. "I got some of your favorite wine if you wanna have a glass."

Lala smiled. "Okay," she said. "I guess." She squinted at Qoree.

As Qoree went into the kitchen to open the wine and pour glasses, he turned and looked at Lala. "So," he said, "who did you say came in there askin' that Sharon chick about me?"

"I don't know," Lala said, going back to sit on the couch. "Some chick named Ronnisha or somethin' like that. I think that was her name, but I don't really know. You know that I ain't been goin' to that shop for too long, although they did do a pretty good job with my hair. So, I don't know if she is a regular or just some chick that came in that day because she knew that Sharon chick."

"Ronnisha, Ronnisha," Qoree said, to himself, trying to see if the chick's name rang a ball. "Naw," he said, shaking his head, "I don't think I know no chick name Ronnisha."

"Yeah, she didn't say she knew you or nothin' like that," Lala said. Qoree came in and handed her a glass of wine. She took a sip then added, "She was askin' the Sharon chick because she said her dude is havin' some sort of get-together and was try'na get in touch with you 'cause you the only nigga or somethin' that he couldn't get in touch with and she was sayin' somethin' like she was just try'na see if Sharon knew you since she be out and about so much, I guess. Trust me, baby, I don't know them females in there and I was just there to get my hair done. I ain't even say nothin', 'cause you know how these niggas be jealous when they find out you know somebody or somethin'. I just sat there quiet and listened to what I could."

"I feel you on that," Qoree said, taking a gulp from his glass then setting it down on the end table next to the couch. He put his hand on Lala's thick, brown thigh. "So, did she say her nigga's name or what?"

"Danez or somethin' like that," Lala answered. "I don't know. I may have heard wrong, but it sounded somethin' like that. Maybe the name was Damon or somethin'. Shit, I don't know."

"Who?" Qoree asked, clearly alarmed. "Danez?"

Lala turned and looked at Qoree. "Yeah," she said. "That's what the chick in Sharon's chair said. And that's when Sharon went on and on about how you used to hang with her cousins. She even knew where you stayed and stuff, or thereabouts. She said somethin' about you would be over to her cousin's house, chillin' and shit, but you lived on White. She didn't really know what part of White, so I wasn't really trippin' about what she was sayin'."

"Danez?" Qoree said. "His chick was up in the salon today?"

"Yeah," Lala said. She sat her glass down on the coffee table. "Why? Why your face look like that? Do you remember when you was cool with him?"

"Cool with him?" Qoree asked. "Man, fuck that nigga. That's the nigga I'm lookin' for right now while he got his bitch goin' around town and askin' about me and thinkin' that I won't hear about it. I got eyes and ears everywhere."

"What?" Lala asked. "How you know him?"

"I don't, really," Qoree said. "But I just put his boy in the hospital for fuckin' around in The Land without even talkin' to me about it first. He next on my list."

"Qoree," Lala said, shaking her head. "You not out there doin' stupid shit still, are you? I mean, don't go causin' no shit."

"Causin' no shit?" Qoree asked. "How the fuck am I causin' some shit? Remember when I had you go to the bedroom the other night while I had that chick Rain over here for some business?"

"Yeah," Lala said, turning away and rolling her eyes. "I remember. I looked out from the bedroom and looked at that chick when she came in the door. Now let me find out you got somethin' goin' on with her and I swear to God it's gon' be hell up in the fuckin' house, for you and for her."

"Naw," Qoree said, shaking his head. "Definitely ain't nothin' goin' on between me and that busted chick. You ten times better lookin' than her. She just doin' me a couple favors. Well, she already did one, so now we just gotta work on the other."

116

Lala, once again, took a long moment to look at Qoree. "Qoree," she said, "is there somethin' you not tellin' me? I mean, I know you out in these streets, doin' what you gotta do to make money and shit, but what you done got yourself involved in this time?"

Qoree looked at Lala, wondering if he could really trust her. At first, like most relationships, he and Lala had basically hooked up with the intentions of just being friends with benefits. However, he soon saw that not only did he like her body, but he also liked her mind. She was good at keeping quiet while also being there for him when he needed to come home to someone. Loyalty was something that he found so hard to find in a woman that when he did, he didn't really know if he could trust it or not. He'd had issues with females in the past.

"You betta not run your mouth if I tell you this shit," Qoree said.

"Run my mouth?" Lala asked. "Who the fuck I'mma tell? You know I don't be out in these streets like that. Shit, I got a few friends, and even them I keep at a distance, 'cause you know how these females be actin' nowadays. What, Qoree? Somethin' is up and I can tell."

"I'm lookin' for that nigga Danez," Qoree said. "He and his boy Lamarcus came in The Land and just started makin' moves and stuff without even talkin' to me and stuff. That's the fucked up thing about it. So, me and my niggas shot that nigga Lamarcus' house up and shit and ran up in there and took what was ours. Now the nigga in the hospital."

"What?" Lala asked, sounding surprised. "Why would you do somethin' like that?"

"What you mean?" Qoree asked. "You can't let these niggas come in on your shit and not send no message. Fuck that nigga. And I'mma get his nigga Danez next, since he wanna have his chick goin' around and askin' about me and shit. And you wasn't sayin' all that when you was helpin' me count all that money the other night."

Lala smiled and looked away, in a very bashful way. "Well," she said, at a loss for words. "I mean, I'mma help you count the money and stuff, you know."

"Yeah, I know," Qoree said. "I know. Ain't that somethin', though? His chick came up in the salon today, huh? What you say her name was again?"

"Ronnisha," Lala answered. "Or, at least, that's how it sounded when she came walkin' through the door and said wassup to Sharon. I was sittin' right there when they started talkin', so I don't think that I misheard nothin'." She paused. "So, you not out there killin' niggas and shit, is you Qoree?"

"No," Qoree said, shaking his head. "You know I'm not gon' kill no nigga unless he start some shit with me and it gotta go that way. I'm just lettin' these niggas know that I'm the one who run The Land, even if them niggas up there in the hood don't hardly ever see me. As far as I'm concerned, they ain't got to never see me. All they got to do is know that I'm there and that they need to respect. Shit, if I had the time and energy, I would get any and every nigga up in there who ever did shit with them niggas Danez and Lamarcus, but I'm bein' nice and just goin' after them."

"Hmm, hmm," Lala answered. "So, what do the Rain chick have to do with all that shit? How the fuck is she even involved?"

Qoree looked at Lala for a moment before he answered. "She is the Lamarcus nigga's chick," he answered. "And I got a little deal with her to where everything will be better off for her if she just help me out. So far, she been doin' alright. She a hoe and stuff, and you know that some niggas love them types."

"Oh, I know," Lala said. "I know."

Qoree thought more and more about how lucky he felt. What were the chances that Lala would just so happen to be sitting in the chair next to Danez's chick? He felt like he almost won the lottery. He also knew that he told Lala enough, or at least as much as she could handle for the moment. Needing to distract her from the topic, he knew it was time to put it down.

"So," Qoree said, "what about what I said early?" He smiled and lowered his eyes.

Lala giggled. She knew exactly what Qoree was talking about, but she liked to play hard to get. "What you talkin' about, Qoree? What about what we said earlier?"

"You know," Qoree said, rubbing Lala's hands aggressively. "When I'mma get some of that pussy? You know how wine get me

118

to feelin' and shit. A nigga's dick get all big and throbbin' and shit." He patted his crotch. "Don't act like you don't want this shit."

Lala took a big gulp of her wine then looked down at Qoree's bulging manhood. She grabbed it with her head, feeling it slowly grow. "I mean," she said, not knowing what to say.

"You mean what?" Qoree asked. "Girl, stop playin' with a nigga and gimme that pussy."

Lala smiled and stood up. Standing in front of Qoree, she pulled her pants down and turned around. Next thing she knew, Qoree had leaned forward and kissed her big, brown ass cheeks as if they were each a million-dollar check with his name written on it and ready to cash. She giggled. "Boy, stop," she said.

"Stop playin' with a nigga," Qoree said. "You know you like that shit. You the one that used to dance and shit, Chocolate Bunny."

It didn't take Lala long to get undressed. She looked back at Qoree. "So, what you sayin'? You want me to go back to dancin'?"

"Fuck, naw," Qoree said. "You betta keep that pussy covered up for a nigga." He slapped her ass again. "I'mma fuck this pussy up so bad like it stole somethin'."

Just then, Qoree stood up and pulled his pants done. Within seconds, he had, while standing, leaned back and planting his palms into the back of the couch. His throbbing hard dick now pointed out toward the middle of the room like a torpedo. Lala shook her ass a little bit before turning around and dropping to her knees. "Damn, nigga," she said. "This dick is hard as rock."

"I told you what that wine be doin' to me," Qoree said. "Now, suck on that rock hard dick. Just suck on it."

Lala did as she was told. She took Qoree's manhood into her mouth and slurped on it as if it were a big chocolate bar. She sped up. At first, Qoree had begun to put his hand on Lala's head, but he stopped himself. If there was one thing he'd learned in life, it was to never mess with a black woman's hair when she'd just gotten it done. Instead, he grabbed the sides of her head and helped to glide her head up and down his shaft. "Fuck," he said. "Chocolate Bunny suckin' on that dick, ain't she?"

Lala nodded her head as her mouth was full of Qoree's meat. "Hmm, hmm," she hummed.

Qoree let Lala suck on his manhood for several more minutes before he stopped her and said, "A nigga is ready for that pussy. Turn around and put that ass on a nigga so he can watch it bounce."

Lala quickly stood up. This position was always her favorite, so she did not hesitate the least bit to get going. Qoree, still standing but leaning back with his hands on the back of the couch, curved his back even more so that his dick was pointing out toward the middle of the room. He watched as Lala turned her thick, chocolate body around. He slapped her ass and told her, "There you go. Sit that pussy on the dick and bounce. Just bounce."

Smiling, Lala leaned over as she backed her pussy up and onto Qoree's manhood. Slowly, she slid down. "Hmm," she moaned, feeling Qoree fill her up. "This feel so good."

"Hmm, hmm," Qoree said, smiling. He looked up at the ceiling. "Shit, this shit feel good."

Lala took a few seconds to get used to Qoree's size. He didn't particularly have a lot of length, but he did have girth. She felt her insides stretch as she lowered herself all the way down to Qoree's pelvis. Once she'd gotten good and comfortable, she bounced up and down. Qoree looked down at her big, round ass jiggling with every up and down motion she made. He pulled one arm up off of the couch and slapped her ass. "Damn, you got a big ass," he said. "Shit, this ass is fat as fuck."

"Hmm, hmm," Lala hummed, nodding. "Just watch that ass bounce up and down. Just watch that ass."

By no means was Lala a hoe, but she did enjoy the attention her ass brought her. She'd been a stripper for a few years at a club in Cincinnati then one in Indianapolis before she met Qoree. However, she'd never gone home with too many men, especially those she'd meet where she worked. That still didn't change how good she felt when a man admired the gift that God had given her: dark skin and an ass that would force even the sexiest chick in porn into early retirement.

Lala now moaned loudly as things were in full swing. The living room filled with the sound of her ass colliding with Qoree's pelvis. At a rhythmic pace, she bounced up and down for several minutes. "Fuck, nigga!" she screamed. "Fuck!"

Not being able to take it anymore, Qoree needed to long-dick her as if it were his last chance. He leaned forward, causing Lala to nearly fall over. He caught her by grabbing her hips. Once his grip was firm, he stroked in and out, going deep and hard.

"Shit, Qoree!" Lala exclaimed. "Yeah, nigga! Fuck that pussy! You gon' make me cum! Shit! You gon' make me cum!"

Qoree nodded, knowing that he was the man. "You like that dick?" he asked, slapping Lala's ass. "You like this fat dick?"

"Yes!" Lala answered, bending all the way over and grabbing her ankles. "Shit, I'm about to cum."

Just then, Qoree watched as Lala became weak. Her legs were starting to feel like jelly to her. To stop her from falling over, Qoree held on even tighter as he pummeled her pussy, knowing that he was going to put her to sleep by the time he was done with her. He continued stroking in and out of Lala, watching the way her ass jiggled like an earthquake in California. "Cum on that dick," he told her. "Go on and come on that fat dick."

Qoree then felt Lala's insides tighten up on his dick. She came, screaming as if it was her first orgasm. "Fuck!" she squealed.

Qoree smiled and slapped her ass again. "I love this pussy," he said. "Fuck, I love this pussy."

Not ready to cum yet, Qoree long stroked Lala for several more minutes. The wine always help him to get his stroke and stamina game up. And Lala sure didn't mind. Within ten minutes, she'd had another orgasm. After about fifteen minutes or so, Qoree himself was ready to blow his load.

"Where you want it?" Qoree asked. "I'm close. Where you want it, Chocolate Bunny? Where you want this nut?"

"I don't care," Lala said. "I don't give a fuck, Qoree. Shit, this dick feel good."

Qoree, feeling his balls draw up close to his body, knew his moment was coming. Holding Lala's hips so hard that even if she wanted to move she wouldn't be able to, he pounded her so hard her ass was starting to sting. His dick throbbed from hearing her scream with curse words slipping out of her lips. "I'm 'bout to drop these kids off in this pussy," he announced, breathing deeply. "Fuck, girl. I'm 'bout to drop these kids off in this pussy."

Qoree let out a deep grown before his body tensed up. He let go inside of Lala, not even thinking about whether or not she was on her birth controls. With his body covered in sweat, beads running down in his face, he slowly stepped back. He and Lala heard the sloshy sound his dick made when it slipped out of her insides. Out of breath, Qoree sat back down on the couch and leaned back. "Shit!" he said.

Lala sat down on the couch next to Qoree. "Shit?" she asked. "I'm the one that is feelin' all sore and shit, nigga."

"Hmm, hmm," Qoree said, closing his eyes for a moment. "I beat that pussy up."

"Sure did," Lala said.

"I almost grabbed that head a couple times too," Qoree said.

"Oh no you didn't," Lala said. "You know betta than that."

Qoree chuckled. "Yeah," he said. "I know, I know."

Qoree and Lala, ready to lie down for a moment, went to the bedroom. In the bed, Qoree had Lala put her head on his chest as they chatted. While talking, Qoree couldn't help but to think about the Sharon chick up at the salon. He looked at the time, seeing that 9 o'clock was coming up. Almost as if Lala had been reading his mind, she looked at him and asked, "What you thinkin' about?"

Qoree hesitated before answered. "Money," he answered. "I don't like them niggas fuckin' with my money."

"I feel you on that," Lala said, smiling. She remembered helping to count the money Qoree had come home with the other night. "You not gon' go after the Danez nigga, are you?"

"Hell yeah," Qoree answered. "Got no choice. You want me to get this money, don't you?"

Lala chuckled and nodded. "Hmm, hmm," she said, clearly drifting off for a late evening nap. She always slept hard after getting some dick. "Just be careful," she said, softly. "Just watch yourself, Qoree."

Chapter 12

Qoree lay in bed and pretended to be falling to sleep until he saw that Lala was breathing steadily. After checking to make sure that she was truly knocked out, by nudging her gently, he slid out from underneath her. Once he'd stood up on the side of the bed, he tapped her shoulder and said, "Baby, I gotta go handle some business. I'll be right back, okay?"

Barely hearing what Qoree said, Lala simply nodded her head. She turned over, mumbling, "Okay."

Qoree went back out into the living room and slid back into his clothes. He grabbed his keys then put on his jacket. His sights were set on the beauty salon, up on 30th Street. If his memory served him well, he remembered a day when he and Lala had been out riding around and doing some shopping. They'd passed the shop and she pointed out how she'd start going there. With the time going on 9 o'clock, he hoped to find Sharon still in the shop so that they could have a little chat.

Qoree hurried out of the house and hopped into his Lincoln. On his way to the shop, he remembered that he hadn't heard from Rain. He smiled, knowing that he had her exactly where he wanted her. "Let that bitch fuck me over and granny is gon' be gone," he said, confidently. He checked his phone a few more times and saw that there was no message from Rain, making a mental note to hit her up when he got out of the shop from talking to Sharon. Part of him wanted to roll up into the hospital and wait on Danez, but that would just be too hood. And too risky, on top of all that.

When Qoree rolled down 30th Street, which was only about a mile and a half or so from where he lived on White, he looked at The Land and thought about how he'd grown up in the area. He'd made so much money that he just couldn't let it go. As the small brick building where the Urban Beauty Salon was located came up, he could see that lights were still on. He smiled, feeling anxious and hoping that Sharon was still in there working.

Slowly, Qoree rolled by the shop. In the few seconds he had to look inside, he saw that Sharon was indeed there. It would have been virtually impossible to miss her bright red hair. After riding around the block, he rolled by again. There seemed to be another woman in the shop, but she was getting stuff together as if she were about to walk out of the door. With that in mind, Qoree pulled into the parking lot at the side of the building. He decided that he'd wait to see if Sharon came outside so he could talk to her in a more private place, in case there were even more women in the shop that he couldn't see from riding by on the street.

Qoree waited several minutes before hearing two females from around the front of the building. It sounded as if they were saying goodbye to one another. As their voices faded, and a door closed, Qoree waited. Within seconds, a plump woman with gray hair came walking around the corner – the other woman that Qoree had seen in the shop when he'd passed by the front of the building. He waited and watched the woman climb into a black Jeep. When she pulled off, he knew that it was show time. Sharon had information that he needed. And he was willing to do whatever it took to get it.

Qoree climbed out of his car and casually walked around the front of the building. When he'd turned onto 30th Street, a hard wind funneled from the west and slammed into his body. He pushed ahead, however, until he was in front of the shop's window. There, he could see Sharon sweeping up around her booth. The other stylists' chairs were empty and the lights above their mirrors were turned off. Quickly, Qoree walked up to the door and pulled it open. Sharon looked up and smiled. "Hey, how you doin'?" she said, not realizing exactly who she was looking at.

"Wassup?" Qoree said coldly but smiling.

Just then, Sharon leaned the broom against the wall. She realized who she was looking at and smiled, thinking that Qoree was looking at her like a piece of meat. She put a bit of an arch in her back as she turned around, knowing that men liked to see her twirl a little bit. Qoree shook his head, seeing the desperation in this woman's face and movements.

"Oh, Qoree?" Sharon asked. "Is that you? I ain't seen you in a minute? How you been?" In all reality, Sharon was taken aback. It was so ironic that he'd come walking in on the very same day that Ronnisha had made an appointment and asked about him while she was getting her hair done. "You know what?" she said. "I was just thinkin' about you, Qoree."

"Oh, was you?" Qoree asked, smirking. He stepped forward and looked down the hallway that led to the back of the building. "You the only one in here?" he asked.

Sharon looked down the hall then back at Qoree, now feeling a little alarmed. She didn't like how Qoree had asked her that question. Something was definitely a little off-putting about him, and she still didn't know exactly what. He didn't have any hair to do, let alone a woman with him that would need her hair done. Why would he be coming into the shop this late in the evening?

"I mean," Sharon said, shrugging, "yeah. The other stylist just left and now I'm cleanin' up so I can head on outta here and get home. What you comin' in here for?"

Qoree stepped closer to Sharon, every so often glancing back at the street. "Let's step in the back real quick so we can have a little talk, if you don't mind," he suggested.

Sharon shook her head, seeing the look on Qoree's face. There was also something about his tone that just didn't sit well with her. "Nigga, who the fuck you think you is," Sharon snapped. "I guess ain't nobody told you about me. I don't just do what some nigga walk in the shop, this late at night at that, and tell me. What the fuck do you want?" She bravely looked him up and down. "I'm not gon' just step in the back because you tell me to, nigga. You got me twisted."

"Okay," Qoree said, realizing this woman didn't know who she was dealing with. "You wanna do it the hard way, then we can. That's coo."

"Do what the hard way?" Sharon asked, confused.

"I heard that somebody came up in here askin' about me, earlier," Qoree said.

Sharon shook her head and looked away. "Naw, nigga," she responded. "I don't know shit about that, so I don't even know why you askin' me. I ain't been talkin' to nobody about you. Why you here for? I know you was pushin' up on me at one time, but I ain't know you was the stalkin' type."

"Bitch, shut the fuck up," Qoree said. "You sound like that dye in your head is gettin' into your brain. Don't nobody want that ole fishy pussy you got. Who the fuck came up in here with my name in they mouth?"

"Nigga, get the fuck outta this shop," Sharon said. She then stepped over to her counter and dug her hand into her pocket. "Before I call the police on you and they show up and shoot a nigga.

Don't think I won't call them. You comin' up in here and startin' shit with me and I ain't got time for that shit."

Sharon pulled her phone out and looked into the screen. Before she knew it, Qoree had stepped over. He wrapped his hand around Sharon's wrist and squeezed as hard as he could, causing her to turn red. She pulled back, but couldn't get free from his grip. "What the fuck is you doin', nigga?" Sharon asked, her Georgia accent coming out in her words. "Get yo hand off of me. I don't know you like that, so why the fuck is you here?"

"Put that phone down," Qoree demanded.

"Nigga, you crazy," Sharon said, shaking her head. Once again, she tried to pull her arm away but was unsuccessful in doing so. "I'm callin' the police."

With a swift and heavy hand, Qoree slapped Sharon across the face. He smiled when he'd heard a gasp slip out of her lips. She looked up at him with cold eyes and screamed, "Get the fuck off me, nigga!"

Qoree, tired of dealing with this difficult woman, slapped Sharon again. This time, he had let go of her wrist then pushed her back. Sharon, who was not as young as she thought or wished she was, feel into the adjacent stylist booth. Upon regaining her balance, she stood up and looked at Qoree. Full of rage, and never being the kind of woman to just let some man have his way with her, she began swinging. Qoree, young and having grown up in the streets, was quick enough to move out of Sharon's way. She did not get a single lick in, only barely breaking the skin on his forearm.

Tired and panting like a thirsty dog, Sharon stopped. "What do you want?" she asked.

Qoree charged forward and wrapped his hand around Sharon's neck. Her eyes bulged. She struggled to breathe and grabbed Qoree's muscular forearm with both hands. "Okay, okay," she said, trying to pull air into her mouth. Fear riveted through her body. "You ain't gotta do this," she said. "You ain't gotta do this."

Qoree chuckled and looked back at the street. "Get in the back so we can talk for a minute without people seein' what you in here goin' through, okay?" he said.

Sharon nodded. "Okay, okay," she said. "Just let go of my neck."

Qoree let up then pushed Sharon toward the hallway. Sharon, fearing for her life, went on to the back. In the kitchen, she backed up against a counter, She wondered when and if Qoree would pull a gun out and end her life. "Don't kill me," she pleaded. "Just don't kill me."

"I'm not gon' kill you, bitch," Qoree said. "What the fuck was that chick Ronnisha askin' you about me for earlier? Huh?"

Sharon quickly pulled the conversation up in her mind, wishing that she'd never opened her mouth. "I mean," she said, "she was just askin' if I knew you. That's all."

"And what you say?" Qoree asked.

"I told her yeah, nigga," Sharon said. "You did used to hang out with my cousins and stuff. That's all I told her."

"Oh," Qoree said, chuckling. He hated how women lied so effortlessly. "That ain't what I heard." He noticed some tools sitting on the floor, next to a patch of the wall that looked as if it had been redone recently. He quickly picked a hammer up, causing Sharon to back up even more.

"What the fuck you about to do with that?" Sharon asked.

Qoree didn't respond to Sharon's question. Rather, he was going to show her. He pointed at the kitchen counter. "Put your hand on the counter," he said. He then noticed how Sharon was hesitating. "Put your hand on the counter before I kill you right here in this kitchen and let your coworkers and shit find you in the morning. Put your hand on the fuckin' counter!"

Murmuring the word *no* over and over again, Sharon closed her eyes. She sweated profusely as she spread her hand out, flat on the counter. Qoree looked into Sharon's pleading eyes. "Why you lyin'?" he asked. "I know you told that bitch where I live...on White. I don't like liars."

Sharon, not knowing what to say, couldn't help but look down at her hand. Just then, Qoree slammed the hammer down onto the upper side of Sharon's hand. She screamed so loud – a scream that would go unheard. "Now, bitch," Qoree said, seeing that he'd gotten his point across. "I need you to help a nigga out, or shit gon' get a lot worse for you. Some niggas been fuckin' with my money and I just can't have that."

Sharon looked into Qoree's eyes, realizing that she was looking into the eyes of a killer.

CPSIA information can be obtained
at www.ICGtesting.com
Printed in the USA
LVOW04s0801030816

498776LV00015B/226/P